TRIPLE CROWN

When owners, trainers and others in
California's horse-racing world begin
receiving anonymous letters, broadcaster
Jerry Brogan is intrigued and brings his
sleuthing talents to bear on the problem.
Then he discovers the body of a racehorse
owner, murdered in complex and bizarre
circumstances, and new doubt is cast on
the supposed suicide of a trainer. Is 'Old
Rosebud', sender of the letters,
responsible, and can he be unmasked
before more deaths ensue?

TRIPLE CROWN

Jon Breen

ATLANTIC LARGE PRINT
Chivers Press, Bath, England.
John Curley & Associates Inc.,
South Yarmouth, Mass., USA.

Library of Congress Cataloging in Publication Data

Breen, Jon L., 1943–
   Triple crown.

   (Atlantic large print)
   1. Large type books.   I. Title.
[PS3552.R3644T7   1986b]   813'.54   85–30773
ISBN 1–55504–025–X

British Library Cataloguing in Publication Data

Breen, Jon L.
   Triple crown.—Large print ed.—(Atlantic
   large print)
   I. Title
   813'.54[F]   PS3552.R3644

   ISBN 0–7451–9136–3

This Large Print edition is published by Chivers Press, England, and
John Curley & Associates, Inc, U.S.A. 1986

Published in the British Commonwealth by arrangement with Macmillan
London Ltd and in the U.S.A. and Canada with Walker & Co

U.K. Hardback ISBN 0 7451 9136 3
U.S.A. Softback ISBN 1 55504 025 X

In Memory of Fred Dannay

TRIPLE CROWN

'He got an Old Rosebud letter in the mail.'

'It's getting to be a status symbol.'

Jerry Brogan almost turned around to ask the two passing racetrack employees what they were talking about. But he didn't, figuring the mystery was probably better than the reality. The Surfside Meadows public-address announcer continued his walk across the vast and empty parking lot, looking forward to breakfast in the backstretch lunchroom.

It was early on an April Friday. Jerry, a year-round publicity consultant of the southern California track, had been away from the office for a week and had deliberately cut himself off from all of his usual contacts in the world of thoroughbred racing, an indulgence he could easily manage a few times a year during the period between Surfside meetings.

The backstretch fast-food outlet, in contrast to the gourmet dining facilities in the frontside clubhouse, had the welcoming look of a clean but slightly run-down truckstop café. It was now kept open year-round because of the large number of horses stabled at Surfside even when the races weren't in session. Some of the trainers, grooms and exercise riders would be able to fill him in on the 'Old Rosebud' business as well as anything else he might have missed. As his bulky form appeared through the door of the lunchroom, Jerry received friendly greetings from many of the horsemen at the tables, but the atmosphere seemed unusually subdued.

Seated at one of the tables was a gnarled exercise rider named Tim Bastian, half Jerry's weight but still too heavy to ride in the afternoon. Jerry sat down to join him.

'What's the matter with everybody?' he asked.

Tim looked up from his muddy cup of black coffee. 'Just heard about Denny Kilbride.'

'What happened to Denny?'

'Dead. Went over a cliff at Surfside Beach late last night.'

'That's awful. Was he driving . . . ?'

'Denny didn't drive. He was walking. They say he fell. Or jumped, if you ask me. He was an unhappy character, Denny Kilbride.'

'I thought his luck was turning better lately, though, what with Questing Willie. He trained him and was part owner, too.'

'It'd take more than one good horse to lift poor Denny's gloom, I can tell you that. He lived under a cloud. Carried it around with him.

'I wonder if they know about this up in the office. I got in early and didn't see anybody up there to talk to.'

Hortense, the platinum-wigged waitress who had been a fixture at Surfside Meadows since the first meeting more than thirty years ago, stopped at the table, ostensibly to take their order. But she was more interested in imparting another piece of information. 'Did you fellas hear the latest on Denny? They say he had an Old Rosebud letter in his pocket when he jumped.'

Tim waved his hand in an impatient gesture. 'That's a bunch of crap.'

'Will somebody please tell me what an Old Rosebud letter is?' Jerry asked.

'You *have* been out of touch,' the waitress exclaimed.

'Why else would I come here, Hortense? Not for the food.'

Tim Bastian chuckled, and Hortense sniffed. Jerry knew her umbrage at the remark was phony. 'They're threatening letters, signed "Old Rosebud",' she said, glad for a fresh audience. 'Lots of big owners and trainers have been getting them.'

'Big like Denny Kilbride?'

Tim shrugged. 'Well, there is Questing Willie. But I don't think they're actually

3

threatening letters, Hortense.'

'They sure are threatening.'

'Have you seen one?'

'Well, no. Have you?'

'No, but what I hear is they're just a prank. Somebody's idea of a good time. No real threat in 'em.'

'That's not what I hear. They've got a lot of people scared out of their wits. And what about Denny Kilbride?'

'If your information's true, Hortense,' the rider said, 'the note prob'ly had nothing to do with his dying.'

'Who's been getting these letters?' Jerry asked.

'All the big-shot owners and trainers,' said Hortense.

'Not what I hear,' said Tim. 'I heard just people with stakes-class three year olds have been getting them.'

Jerry was beginning to doubt he would get much definite information this way. But he tried another question. 'Why are the letters signed "Old Rosebud"? Somebody see *Citizen Kane* once too often?'

'Citizen who? I don't know anything about that,' said Tim.

'It was a movie with Orson Welles,' Hortense said, with a boastful note at this further display of knowledge.

'This goes back a lot farther than any Orson Welles. Haven't you people heard of Old Rosebud? Clyde!' The rider beckoned to a backstretch octogenarian at another table. 'Tell these folks about Old Rosebud. The horse, I mean.'

'Great horse!' the elderly man obliged in a booming voice that carried across the room. 'Won the 'fourteen Kentucky Derby in two/o-three and two-fifths, record time then. Johnny McCabe rode him. Hodge second, Bronzewing third. Didn't run at four or five but came back to be handicap champ in 'seventeen. He was still running as an eleven year old in 'twenty-two. Won forty out of eighty lifetime starts. Hell of a horse. Not many people remember him. Guess somebody does, though.'

By the time his breakfast was over, Jerry knew plenty about *that* Old Rosebud, but very little about his current letter-writing namesake.

★   ★   ★

That evening, after a grueling twenty-five minutes of driving north on the San Diego Freeway, Jerry pulled his car into the driveway of the Tokyo Armadillo restaurant, the site of Bill and Arleen Holman's party. A white-jacketed youth swung his door open, and Jerry maneuvered his oversized frame out of the driver's seat. He hated valet parking as much as he hated going to parties alone, but Bill and Arleen were old friends and there would be no shortage of other old friends.

The Holmans seemed to have taken over the whole restaurant and invited enough guests to fill it. Not seeing his hosts and not being asked for his invitation, Jerry wandered in, nodding and waving to many familiar members of the local turf set. He was drawn immediately to the generous and varied supply of food at the long buffet table and was eating a puffed-pastry concoction called a *fuilletée au fromage* when a much shorter and less bulky man walked over to him with arm outstretched.

'Ab,' said Jerry with pleasure. 'I didn't know you'd be here.'

'I hoped *you* would be,' said Abner Kelly. 'Our old school chum has made it big, hasn't he?'

'To our immediate benefit. Try one of these. They're great.' Jerry consumed the last bite of pastry and gulped a swallow of champagne.

'Are those Japanese?'

'More like French. They have a versatile chef.'

'I had some tempura but I can't find any sushi.'

'I've been trying to avoid that stuff all my life. Sushi or not, this is quite a spread. What do you think it's costing Bill and Arleen?'

'I don't even like to think about it.'

Bill Holman, who had gone to college with Jerry and Ab, was the owner of Tall Sequoia, a three-year-old colt who had recently won the Santa Anita Derby and was ticketed for Kentucky.

'Has it occurred to you,' Jerry mused, 'that you, a network executive, and I, a widely known track announcer, are probably the least eminent people here?'

Ab laughed. 'Speak for yourself. I'm eminent as all hell, and I'm about to make *you* more eminent.'

'Eminent's nice, but I'd settle for rich. What's on your devious mind, Ab?'

'We managed to snatch the TV and radio rights to the Triple Crown races this year.'

'That's great. I knew you had the TV, but I thought the other guys always had the Triple Crown radio.'

'Not this year. It's ours, and all we need is someone to announce them for us. For TV we're committed by contract to use Grant Engle, a pompous ass but competent. For radio, though, who does the call is a lot more

7

important and we want the job done right. Engle doesn't really do a radio call. Hardly anybody does. We want somebody who can call the races *and* do the pre-race commentary, a one man team. I, of course, told my leaders that I know a guy who is just the person they want. Born into racing, knows it inside out, a cross between Vin Scully and Joe Hernandez, works cheap. . .'

Jerry blurted, 'I'll do it!' He knew he should have been more nonchalant—overeagerness could only damage his bargaining position—but he also knew he'd never seen a Kentucky Derby, Preakness or Belmont anywhere but on TV, and this was an opportunity he couldn't pass up. 'What does it pay?'

'Jerry, if we just paid your transportation and expenses to those three events, you'd be doing very well.'

'But that's not all. You also pay a generous fee, right?'

'"Generous", of course, is a relative term. Look, just give me the word you're interested, and I'll have somebody get in touch with you about the messy details like money, OK?'

'Right. And tell them I'm weighing other offers.'

'Very funny. But I'll keep it neutral—I won't tell them you practically licked my hand when I mentioned Triple Crown.'

Jerry saw Abner's eyes light up as he waved to someone over Jerry's shoulder. Arleen Holman was drifting toward their corner of the large room.

'Hi. You know you guys look like Laurel and Hardy from a distance?' she said.

'I told you you shouldn't have grown that mustache, Ab,' Jerry kidded. In fact he outweighed Kelly by a hundred pounds and was in no doubt which of them was the Hardy half.

Arleen was a dark-haired, dark-eyed beauty in her early thirties. But even when she smiled a permanent set of forehead lines gave her a worried look. Though she was doing her best to mingle with her guests, she obviously wasn't happy.

'This is terrific,' Abner said. 'It's nice to know such successful people.'

'Sure,' she said ruefully. 'But sometimes success can be almost as nerve-racking as poverty.'

'Except that you eat better,' Jerry pointed out.

'If I see myself in one more newspaper story with "rags-to-riches" in the headline ... I don't mind feeding you guys, but who are the rest of these people? Bill seems to think his last name is Whitney or Vanderbilt. Tall

9

Sequoia is just one horse.'

'One horse that'll be worth umpteen million dollars in syndication rights if he wins a Triple Crown event,' Jerry said.

'If, if, if. How many Santa Anita Derby winners get that far?'

'Quite a few,' Jerry insisted, not sure of the numbers but always ready to boost West Coast racing.

Bill Holman had separated himself from a circle of regulars from the LA *Times* society page and was now drifting their way, waving his drink periodically at guests as he passed. He reached the trio with a sign of relief.

'I don't even recognize some of these people,' he said.

'I thought they were your pals,' Arleen said sourly.

'Maybe this wasn't such a good idea,' Bill said, picking up his wife's mood. 'It started out as a little get-together for a few close friends—'

'—and then you decided a few close friends included half the membership of the Santa Anita turf club. If you'd invited a hundred and fifty from the backstretch, that would be more like it. They're our people, Bill. Not this bunch.'

Sparks flew between them. Jerry felt a strong desire to absent himself. Watching a

10

couple snipe at each other in public was hardly
ever fun, and the Holmans were ordinarily a
Madison Avenue endorsement of marital
bliss. Being sudden media celebrities was
taking its toll on them.

Arleen smiled and looked at her guests
apologetically. 'I don't know what's the
matter with me,' she said. 'Life in the fast lane
must be getting to me, huh?'

Bill put his arm around her. 'You and me
both, honey. I just got carried away with
inviting people. But you guys would have
been here if it had been a party of ten. So how
goes it, Jerry? Couldn't Donna make it
tonight?'

'No,' he said. Most of his friends had
expected him to be married to the Chicana
drama teacher by now, and so had he. It was
hard to explain why they weren't and he
didn't try. 'Abner here just gave me
something to do between now and when
Surfside opens. I'll be broadcasting the Triple
Crown races—pending final negotiations, of
course.'

'That's wonderful, Jerry,' said Arleen.
'Does that mean you'll be working with
Howard Cosell?'

'No, ABC's not doing it this year. And,
anyway, this is radio.'

'Oh,' she said, with something of a letdown

11

in her voice. It was a reaction Jerry would get accustomed to in the days to come. 'They still do it on the radio, huh?'

'Radio is where the art of broadcast sports reporting is at its highest esthetic level,' Abner assured them, sounding as if he'd memorized the line.

'And compensated commensurately, I hope,' Jerry put in.

'With the greatest compensation of all: professional satisfaction.'

Jerry snorted. 'To make a profit, I'll have to get a bet down on Tall Sequoia.'

'Better make it to show,' said Arleen.

'You don't believe in him, either?' Bill rebuked her, as lightly as he could manage. The statement seemed to get under his skin far more effectively than her remarks about patrician guests. 'I get so sick of these Easterners making cracks about California racing.'

'I know,' said Jerry. 'All those horses are sprinters and all the tracks are made out of pasteboard and run downhill. In the last few years we've resurfaced some of our tracks to make them as boring as any of the ones on the eastern seaboard, but the Belmont–Aqueduct crowd still spout the same clichés.'

'That's just what I mean,' he said, looking accusingly at his wife.

'Look, fellas,' she said, 'the last time I was an Easterner I didn't know which end of a horse ate the hay, but I don't think it's realistic to expect any horse to beat Gotham City...'

'Gotham City!' Bill echoed. 'What a perfect name for the darling of the New York provincials. I can prove to you by comparison of form against common opponents that Gotham City doesn't belong on the same track with Tall Sequoia!'

'How? Gotham City is undefeated.'

'We beat Pepperpot by four lengths at Anita, and Gotham City only beat him by a length in Florida, that's how!'

Jerry reflected that he could use a chain of opponents to prove Slippery Rock could beat Notre Dame in football, but he decided not to say it.

Arleen said, 'I think we'd be better off if we didn't even go to Kentucky, just ran Sequoia at Hollywood Park instead.'

'Hollywood Park?' Bill said. 'Arleen, people go all their lives without getting a horse with a shot at the classics.'

'But is it worth it?' She lowered her voice. 'Is it worth getting threatening letters in the mail?'

Bill looked uncomfortably at their guests and essayed an unconvincing laugh. 'Forget about that nonsense. It's just some crazy crank.'

'You mean Old Rosebud?' Jerry said softly.

'You've heard about that?' Arleen said.

'I'm afraid it's all over the backstretch. Accounts of it vary wildly, however. Maybe you can tell me. . .'

'I don't really want to talk about that stuff,' Bill said.

'Why, if it doesn't worry you?' Arleen said, with a slight shrillness in her voice.

'It doesn't, but I don't want who's doing it to get a lot of attention.' He looked at Abner and Jerry apologetically. 'I don't mean I think you guys are going to go to the papers and TV about it, but I just think it's better to talk about it as little as possible.'

'It may get in the media now,' Jerry said. 'The scuttlebutt at the track this morning was that Denny Kilbride had one of these letters in his pocket.'

'Denny Kilbride!' said Arleen. 'And he had a good three year old, too, Bill.'

'Questing Willie's nothing but a sprinter. He led the Santa Anita Derby for seven furlongs, but he was lucky to hang on for third.'

'Nevertheless, Denny Kilbride had hopes for him. He thought he was a Triple Crown contender and—'

'Arleen, we can't panic over this stuff. It's all bullshit, and it's not going to stop Tall Sequoia from fulfilling his destiny. He's not only going to Kentucky, but he's going to Maryland and then on to New York to lick Gotham City on his own home ground. That's what he's going to do.'

'Or how could you face all your new friends?' Arleen shot back at him.

Bill shook his head as if to clear the cobwebs. 'I think I ought to go face a few of them now. Excuse me, guys.'

They watched his stocky body retreat into the crowd, still waving and smiling if in a slightly more restrained manner.

Arleen seemed to be fighting back tears. She looked at Abner and attempted a joke. 'Do you think a rags-to-riches thoroughbred family would make a good soap opera? Of course, you'd have to keep them from switching back to rags. That would kill the ratings.' She managed another worried smile and excused herself before Jerry could ask her for any more details about Old Rosebud.

Another guest, who had been surreptitiously enjoying the conjugal exchange from a distance, drifted over to Jerry and Abner. 'Dear, dear,' said Les Randall. 'What a pity some people have so much trouble enjoying success.'

'Hi, Les,' said Jerry. The British journalist, who was doing a seemingly endless series on American racing for one of the lesser London papers, irritated Jerry profoundly but seemed impossible to avoid. 'Do you know Abner Kelley? This is Les Randall.'

'Pleasure. Jerry, I keep telling you, it's pronounced *Lezz*, not *Less*. Short for Leslie.'

Jerry considered extricating himself and getting something more to eat.

'I didn't hear all of that,' Randall said. 'They most inconsiderately lowered their voices there toward the end. But, you know, they sound just like the Gotham City lot.'

'What do you mean?' Ab asked.

'Van Ness Masterton and his wife are always having a go, too.'

'The Holmans aren't "always having a go",' Jerry objected.

'Hey, come on,' said Abner. 'You're keeping me from the gossip. Why do the Mastertons disagree?'

'Well, in this case, *he's* the conservative, fiscally responsible one and *she's* the sport. He plans to retire the horse, sound or not, immediately after the Triple Crown series. With everything Gotham City has accomplished already, he could get a syndicate deal that would put all previous in the shade. She, on the other hand, is determined that

16

they continue to race the horse, at least through his four-year-old season.'

'I can't imagine Van Ness Masterton letting anyone tell him how to run his stable,' said Abner.

'She's doing her best. Do you know her? Charming woman. Could be his daughter, of course. Third wife for him, isn't it?'

Jerry didn't doubt that Randall had the number of wives at the tip of his fingers. He often wondered what the British journalist's copy must look like. Closest American equivalent to the lower-class English dailies would be something like the *National Enquirer* or its clone, the *National Onlooker*. Of course, there really wasn't an American equivalent to the really good English papers.

Jerry managed to sneak away, as inconspicuously as a man of his conspicuous size could, leaving Ab Kelley and Les Randall to exchange confidences. He didn't want to mention anything in the writer's presence about the Old Rosebud letters—whatever they were—and hoped Ab wouldn't, either. Still, it was hard to imagine that Randall with all his contacts didn't already know about them.

Though the scene of Bill and Arleen had put a slight damper on his mood, Jerry was still excited at the prospect of seeing and reporting on the Triple Crown series. And by

17

all indications it should be a good one. Regional lines had never been so clearly drawn, with Gotham City carrying the flag of the Easterners, Tall Sequoia of the Californians and other possible starters representing Canada, Washington State, the South, and the Middle West.

Seeing a sliding door to the patio area adjoining the restaurant's main room, Jerry tried to duck out for some fresh air and a look at a pond full of multicolored Koi fish, but before he could get there he was intercepted by a man whose face was familiar. Familiar not just to him but to all America.

'Jerry, how are ya? How are ya? Great to see ya, great. Look, can we talk a second?' Martin Fine looked worried. In his weekly role as the crusading Dr Paul Ames, taking on a different social issue in each episode, looking worried was his speciality.

'Why don't we step out on the patio?' Jerry suggested resignedly. The TV actor was a nice guy but one who tired other people out, which (coupled with his inexplicable small-screen attractiveness to audiences of all ages and sexes) may have accounted for his considerable show-business success, both as performer and producer. Knowing he was giving the actor an opening, he said, 'You look worried, Martin.'

18

'Nah, nah, everything's fine. Top of the world. But look, Jerry, what can you tell me about the requirements to start a horse in the Kentucky Derby? I mean, I thought you just paid your money and I paid my money—two hundred bucks to nominate, and I'm ready to throw in another ten grand to enter him race week and another ten grand to start, probably because I'm crazy—but now somebody says that paying your money's not enough. You know, I'm pretty new to racing. Doc Paul is the first horse I ever owned, and I don't know all the ins and outs. So what can you tell me about it? I'd ask my trainer, but he isn't here, and when I hear something that I don't know about I need to find out right away or I won't sleep, 'cause I'm not one of these guys who takes pills to sleep, no matter what kind of insomnia I get. I don't go for chemical help, not even booze. We did a show on that, great show. But what I want to know from somebody I can trust not to blab it around is what does a horse need to get in the Derby—except a saddle and a jockey, huh?'

Fine took a breath, and Jerry jumped in: 'Well, most years you just pay your fees and enter your horse. But they do limit the field to twenty starters, and lately there have been more than that many wanting to go almost every year, so they have to pare down the field

19

on the basis of earnings.'

'Yeah, sure, earnings. But Doc Paul has won me plenty. Almost three hundred grand. But somebody told me that may not be enough. I don't get it. How many three year olds have earned three hundred grand already, Jerry? Not twenty, huh?'

'Well, here's the thing, Martin. Under the current rules, they only count money won in non-restricted races, and Doc Paul earned his biggest purse in a race that was only for colts bred in California. Without his earnings in Cal-bred races, he may not have enough.'

'But that's not fair at all, Jerry. California-breds are some of the best horses in the world.'

'Not the point, Martin. It's the same for races for Kentucky-breds only—or Canadian–breds or Maryland-breds or Florida-breds or Washington-breds or any-other-breds.'

'So Doc Paul might not be able to start? Jerry, I've got my plans all made for Louisville. It isn't fair.'

'Relax. There may not be enough horses entered for the earnings even to enter the picture this year. Gotham City figures to be an overpowering favorite, and he may scare a lot of the competition off.'

Martin Fine shook his head. 'I don't know. I can't imagine anybody passing up the chance of seeing his horse running in the Kentucky Derby, the most famous race in the world. Gosh, I wish I'd known that about the earnings. I have a lot to learn about racing, Jerry, and that trainer of mine doesn't tell me anything. Sometimes I have the feeling he just thinks of me as the noodnik who pays the bills. If I knew more about it, I'd train the horse myself. Do it yourself, that's my motto. Jerry, if Doc Paul goes, what do you think of his chances?'

Jerry tried to outline a diplomatic response. The little colt had won his only stakes victory at odds of 40–1; and his other races, including a seventh-place finish in Tall Sequoia's Santa Anita Derby, did not suggest that victory had been anything but a lucky fluke. 'Everybody has a chance in a horse race.'

'Yeah, that's what I thought you'd say. We'll show you, Doc Paul and me. We'll show 'em all.' He looked back in at the party through the sliding glass doors. 'I love racing, Jerry, and I love these people. I love being a part of it. Not like the phony Hollywood crowd, I can tell you that.'

Looking at the standing groups of drinkers, Jerry wondered how much difference there could be between this party and a Hollywood party. Could the latter actually provide more phonies? Jerry hadn't been to many

21

Hollywood parties.

'I think I'll give that to the writers,' Martin Fine said.

'Huh?' once again Jerry had failed to follow the actor's mercurial train of thought.

'It's a great murder-mystery plot. Guy like me who wants his horse in the Derby. Twenty-first on the list. Does something to eliminate one of the contenders.'

'Sneaks into the stable area and kills the favorite?'

'Kills the favorite?' Fine seemed shocked. 'No, no, Jerry. People would never go for that. Animal lovers would flood us with protests, and I don't want any cruelty to animals on my show. And it is my show, and I control it. I am in command. Kill a horse on my show? No way. Somebody kills the *owner*.'

'The owner?'

'Sure, the owner of the favorite. Two days before the race. The heirs, out of respect, scratch the horse, right?'

'I don't know. They might let the horse run as a memorial to the owner. I can just hear somebody saying "Old Joe would have wanted it that way." It sounds risky.'

Martin Fine snapped his fingers. 'Wait a minute! Let's say the death of the owner creates some doubt as to who the horse belongs to. Conflicting claims. Somebody challenging the will. With the horse's ownership in doubt, the executors have no choice but to scratch the horse. In comes number twenty-one on the list, and he wins the race.'

'For his TV-star owner?'

Martin laughed. 'No, Jerry, this is fiction. I think I'll get a writer to work on that idea, though. Maybe two writers, working independently, see what they come up with. Thanks for the information, pal. So, look, what's new with you, huh?' His worry temporarily assuaged, the actor put a dime in the fish-food dispenser and started throwing pellets to the multi-colored Koi. They almost climbed out of the water, jumping on top of each other going after the food.

'I just got some great news, Martin. I'll be doing the Triple Crown races on the radio this year.'

'On the radio? Hey, I used to work in radio, tail end of network radio drama in the early fifties. It was great. Nothing like it. No lines to learn, but you couldn't rattle the paper. Do you actually get to go to the race?'

Jerry gaped. 'I assume so. How else could I call it?'

'I thought maybe it was a re-creation, the way they used to do the ball games on the radio back in the forties and fifties.

Remember those days? That was great. Phony crowd noises, bat hitting the ball, all kinds of sound effects. Announcer sitting in the studio reading the teletype and pretending he was at the game. That was terrific. But you'll actually be there, huh?'

'I'll be there, and if you see Ab Kelley tonight don't give him any ideas.'

Martin Fine laughed. 'I get you. Thanks for talking to me, Jerry. I'm straight now, not worried about Doc one bit. Besides, we'll have a chance or two to up his bankroll before Derby time, won't we?'

'Sure, Martin. By the way, there's something I'm curious about that you might be able to clear up for me. Old Rosebud.'

'It was his sled,' the actor said quickly, with a nervous laugh.

'No, not in *Citizen Kane*. A lot of people have been getting anonymous letters signed "Old Rosebud", or that's as much as I've been able to piece together. People with three-year-old contenders. Did you get one?'

'Jerry, I get so much crazy mail, you have no idea.'

'You're holding out on me, Martin.'

'OK, OK! Yeah, I got one. A crazy kook, that's all. He does them by computer, you know. Ugly dot-matrix print on cheap paper. A computer poison-pen writer. But it's all a big joke, Jerry. Nobody takes it seriously.'

'Do you remember what the letter said, Martin?'

'Not exactly. Subtle hint that I'll be blown away if I start Doc Paul in the Derby. But death threats are nothing new to me. When you take on the issues like we do on the show, Jerry, lots of people get mad at you and try to scare you off. You have no idea. But Old Rosebud, whoever the pitiful character is, doesn't scare me a bit. See you in Louisville, huh?' He threw a last handful of fish food toward the center of the pond, sending the Koi sprinting, then slapped Jerry's shoulder and disappeared through the sliding door into the swarms of guests.

Leaning against the patio railing, Jerry reflected that the bundle-of-nerves actor was taking a more sensible approach to this letter-writing campaign than anybody. The death of Denny Kilbride made it seem a bit more sinister, but the old trainer, who'd been trying to hang on at the major California tracks for several years with marginal racing stock after enjoying some success at county fair meetings, had always seemed a prime candidate for suicide, his melancholia too deep to overcome even by a mildly promising three year old.

And Jerry had other things to chew on. What kind of a vantage point would he have at the Derby? It would be tough to call the finish if he wasn't right on the line, and this was one race he had better be sure not to muff. He'd have to find out.

Then it occurred to him he should call Donna with the news. Maybe she'd even like to come to Louisville with him, though paying her expenses would probably wipe out whatever pittance the radio people were going to pay him. He could use the phone here or, better yet, he could find his hosts, say the proper polititudes and go home. That sounded good.

*   *   *

In lighter traffic it was a fifteen-minute drive to Jerry's beachfront home in Surfside. He looked at his watch and saw that it was still early enough to call Donna Melendez on a Friday night. Of course, he had asked her to come to the Holmans' party with him, but she had had another engagement. She was playing mixed doubles in a faculty tennis tournament at Richard Henry Dana High School. The rules indicated a teacher could bring in a partner from outside the faculty, but Jerry Brogan did not navigate a tennis court to her satisfaction or his own.

It seemed sports were always coming
26

between them. Her once fervent misgivings about his involvement in thoroughbred racing—just short of a blood sport in her view—had somewhat moderated, but she was given to physical exercise of a type and intensity he didn't want to share: tennis, skiing, surfing. Jerry had been a high-school interior lineman and a college wrestler, so wasn't unathletic, but he resisted games that emphasized the kind of agility the compact Donna had in abundance. He thought they made his bulky form appear even more ridiculous than usual. A particularly disastrous session at an aerobics class had brought things to a head.

'Hello.'

'Hi, Donna. How did the big tournament go?'

'It was a fiasco. I played with Joe Montgomery, the biology teacher.'

'I remember him. An Adonis. You must have been a beautiful couple.'

'Oh, we were beautiful all right, up till the match started. But he's uncoordinated. His only use in a sport is as a uniform model. To give you an idea of how bad it was, *you* couldn't have done any worse.'

Jerry cringed. 'Well, I hope you had a good time anyway.'

'I had a lousy time. Joe is a vain, strutting

peacock. At least he was willing to try, though.'

Here we go again, Jerry told himself. 'A guy like that looks a lot better looking bad than I do. Look, Donna, not to change the subject, but I want to change the subject. I got some great news tonight.'

'Yeah? What's that?'

'I'm going to do the Triple Crown races on the radio.'

'Oh.' She paused. 'Jerry, that's just great. Uh, what are the Triple Crown races? Is that like the America's Cup, or is it stock cars, or . . . ?'

'Donna, are you putting me on?' He honestly wasn't sure. 'It's the Kentucky Derby, the Preakness and the Belmont Stakes, the three biggest races for three year olds. And I'm going to call them on the radio.'

'You mean it's horses?'

'Yeah, horses. When did I start calling yachts or cars or greyhounds or horned toads? Of course it's horses.'

'OK, OK! Don't get excited.'

'I am excited. It's a great opportunity for me. And I thought maybe you'd like to come to the Derby with me.'

'Oh, Jerry, that's really great of you. You know I'd like to, but it's tough to get away during the school year. When is it?'

'The first Saturday in May. Always.'

'And it's in Kentucky?'

'Yeah, that's why they call it the Kentucky Derby. It's in Kentucky.'

'Jerry, is something bothering you? There's a certain note in your voice. A certain subtle edge. We drama teachers learn to detect little nuances like that.'

Jerry paused and tried to recover his good humor, well aware that the edge in his voice wasn't the least bit subtle. 'Oh, I don't know. I got what I thought was a great piece of news, and nobody seems impressed with it. I mean, I know this isn't the era of Graham MacNamee and Ted Husing, but still...'

'Who are they?'

'Never mind. Look, can I see you tomorrow afternoon? We can talk about it then.'

'Sure, I was hoping to get in some jogging. Want to join me?'

'If you'll join me for my sport later on.'

'Horse racing?'

'No, wrestling!'

★   ★   ★

The weekend passed pleasantly and uneventfully. Aside from scanning the morning papers for an account of Denny Kilbride's death, finding it attributed to accident or suicide with no mention of any mysterious note in the trainer's pocket, Jerry didn't make any attempt to extend his knowledge of the Old Rosebud letters. It kept coming into his mind, though, even as he and Donna were puffing through the park. (Truthfully, she wasn't really puffing much. She didn't even have the good taste to sweat very much.)

On Monday morning, Jerry thought of another way to appease his curiosity. He dialed the Surfside Police Department. The racetrack crowd could provide only rumors, but Lieutenant Wilmer Friend could provide some facts.

'Not much to it, Jerry. A couple of frightened teenagers found Kilbride's body on the rocks at two in the morning. That's quite a drop from the top of the cliff, and there's not much doubt the fall killed him. Everybody said he walked up there a lot. They also said he'd been despondent...'

'For about ten years that I know of,' Jerry said.

'Anyway, it could be suicide or an accidental fall. No reason to suspect anything more sinister than that. No reason at all.'

'I can't help thinking if he was going to kill himself he'd have done it long before now. Wilmer, there's a rumor around the track that he had a letter in his pocket. A letter signed "Old Rosebud".'

Brief silence on the other end of the line. 'How'd anybody know about that?'

'You were keeping it a secret, huh? Then, you must suspect—'

'No, it's no secret. But nobody asked us. Well, nobody asked *me* anyway. Somebody probably talked too much to an acquaintance at the racetrack.'

'What was in this letter?'

'I wouldn't call it a letter. A little statement about front-runners having to eat dirt. And signed "Old Rosebud".'

'Sounds like a threat.'

'No more threatening than some fortune cookies I've read.'

'It was on computer paper? Typed out by a dot-matrix printer?'

'Why are you asking? You seem to know all about it.'

'Wilmer, can your technicians identify an individual computer printer by peculiarities in type, the same as you can a typewriter?'

'I don't really know, but I doubt it. Seems to me I read the other day they're still working on telling one company's printer from another, let alone one individual machine from another. But we aren't really working on it. Should we be? Have there been other notes like this?'

'Yes, but the recipients probably haven't been reporting them to the police.'

'Maybe they should. That's if they expect us to do anything about it. Sounds like a bunch of crap to me, though. Of course, I have an open mind. But I also have a heavy caseload, and I just don't see Denny Kilbride's death as anything but accident or suicide.'

'Oh, I don't, either,' Jerry said casually. 'Just curious, that's all. Old Rosebud was a famous racehorse of the World War I era, won the Kentucky Derby and lots of other big races.'

'Do tell,' Friend said without perceptible interest.

'Maybe our pal with the home computer would be scarier if he'd picked the name of another gelding that came along a few years after Old Rosebud.'

'Who was that?' Friend asked, providing Jerry with the line he wanted.

'Exterminator.'

PRE-RACE 2

Gotham City, a perfectly formed chestnut who looked exactly like the champion he was, stood in his stall at Aqueduct and looked at his human visitors without great interest. His trainer Horace Nurock he knew and trusted. His owners he didn't recognize, but he was seldom upset by strangers. He saw a lot of them, more than ever since his win in the Wood Memorial a few days before. Though he didn't know what the race was called or how much it was worth—he ate every day regardless—he had enjoyed the run.

Horace Nurock bore the visiting delegation with more apprehension. Van Ness Masterton knew enough about horses to be his own trainer and, even tempered as he seemed on the surface, he could be one mean bastard when roused. He made Horace nervous. Acton Schoolcraft was worth a billion dollars and seemed to have a lot of influence over Masterton. He made Horace even more nervous. Carol Masterton was a pampered beauty of forty who looked twenty in the right light. She made Horace horny and nervous. But Horace didn't look either. He couldn't afford to. He looked quiet and capable and was what the papers called 'unflappable'.

'A beautiful animal,' said Schoolcraft. He was a corpulent, red-faced man of seventy-five who talked in a barely audible wheeze. 'Magnificent.'

'Never taken an unsound step in his life,' Horace said.

Van Ness Masterton, a trim and athletic sixty-one, squinted at his trainer. 'I'm superstitious enough that I try to avoid saying things like that. It's true, though.'

'He could be syndicated for millions right now,' said Schoolcraft. 'After the Triple Crown, there's just no telling.'

'That's just when there will be telling,' said Masterton. 'The Belmont will be his last start, come what may. He'll retire an undefeated Triple Crown winner. If they'd just done that with Seattle Slew, can you imagine . . . ?'

'Slew's done all right, on the track and at stud, too,' said Mrs Masterton.

Van Ness glared at her but said nothing. He wasn't gauche enough to say out loud that running the racing stable was none of her business, though that was his unspoken belief. She was from a multi-generation racing family and knew the ins and outs of thoroughbreds as well as he.

'What if he doesn't win the Triple Crown, Van?' she asked him. 'What then?'

'He will. And if he doesn't... Well, I'll syndicate him anyway and wish I'd done it sooner. Can you imagine the money...?'

Carol laughed. 'None of us has to imagine money, do we, Mr Schoolcraft? I'd say we've got plenty. I understand we're paupers by your standards, but we have enough.'

'No such thing,' Schoolcraft replied, with a wheezing laugh.

Van Ness Masterton turned back to his trainer. 'Which race are we going to use for a prep for him in Kentucky?'

Horace ventured an opinion. 'The Derby Trial is over the Churchill Downs track, so that might do him more good. It's a full week before the Derby now, of course, better than when it was Tuesday of Derby week.'

'The Blue Grass at Keeneland is worth more, though, in money and prestige,' said Acton Schoolcraft.

'Right, said Masterton. 'Then, it's Keeneland. Four more races for Gotham City and I can quit holding my breath and let the investors worry.'

'Couldn't we at least keep him in training until the end of the year?' Carol asked, not for the first time. 'Give him a chance to show he can carry a little weight and then take on older horses in the Woodward, the Jockey Club Gold Cup and the Breeders' Cup. You can't assume Horse of the Year for a colt who retires in mid-June.'

'You damn well can if he's an undefeated Triple Crown winner!' Masterton snapped, sick of the argument. 'I know what I'm doing, Carol, and this is a business venture, not a country point-to-point. You just concentrate on our Derby-week party, all right?'

'Ah, yes,' said Schoolcraft, seemingly oblivious to any bad vibrations between the Mastertons. 'I always look forward to that event. What will the quiz involve this year, Van?'

'Haven't decided,' said Masterton, with a slight smile. 'But it'll be tougher than ever.'

'I was beaten last year by some young upstart,' Schoolcraft told Carol. 'Have to get my revenge. The Masterton farm party should be all the more festive this year, with a Masterton colt favored for the Derby. It's been wonderful every year, of course, regardless of hostess, but I know you'll make it a special pleasure, Carol.'

'I'll try,' she said, putting the argument aside for the moment. It would be her first effort at hosting the famous Masterton gala, having become Van's third wife only some ten months before. She accepted such social functions as being in her sphere of responsibility, but the charm of the Masterton farm outside Lexington lay more in the white fences and green bluegrass and barns of expensive thoroughbred stock than anything that went on inside the lavishly furnished house. When she'd married Van she had thought he was a man as steeped in the sporting traditions of racing as she, even to the extent of challenging his annual Derby-week guests with racing trivia games. Why was he so anxious for a quick syndication of Gotham City? He couldn't need the money, could he?

The group moved on to look at a few of the other Masterton horses in Horace Nurock's barn. They included several winners of graded-stakes events and one six-year-old mare who'd won a million dollars in purse money, but with Gotham City only stalls away these were strictly spear-carriers.

Nurock was relieved to see the trio move on. He had another of those anonymous letters in his pocket, received this morning: 'FOREGO THE TRIPLE CROWN, THAT ANCIENT TITLE, OR YOU'LL FIND I'M ARMED—OLD ROSEBUD.' He would have to tell Masterton about it later in the day, but he had strict instructions not to mention the threatening letters around Mrs Masterton or Schoolcraft.

★　　★　　★

37

Bill Holman, opening his morning mail a few thousand miles to the west, said, 'I'll be damned.'

'Another one of those letters?' said Arleen fearfully.

'No, no, we won't see any more of those, honey. The nut's gotten tired.' He passed the engraved invitation across the table to her. 'We've been invited to the Masterton party.'

'You say that like it was something special. What's the Masterton party?'

'Every year Van Ness Masterton has a big Derby-week shindig at his farm in Lexington. And we're invited.'

'Hey,' she said cynically, 'you mean *we* get a chance to freeload for once? Instead of us giving away liquor, somebody gives away liquor to us? It sounds terrific.'

Bill looked at her sadly. 'What's happening to us, Arleen?'

'Great things. We're joining the jet set.'

'Don't you want to go? You know, Masterton owns Gotham City...'

'I should know that.'

'I think it's quite a nice sporting gesture to invite us to come to the party. It's not as if we're old-line Eastern horse people, and I imagine that's who make up most of the guest list.'

'They want a couple of California curios to put on display. They probably invite a select few every year so they can rag them about their sprinters and make fun of their peculiar customs. If anybody wants you to take them on in a mint julep contest, you turn them down, Bill.'

'Then, you'll go?'

She smiled, relenting. 'Of course I'll go, honey. And I'm sorry if I'm being a bitch. This can't go on forever, and we might as well try to enjoy it. But we have to realize it all has to end some time.'

'Why does it have to?'

'Very simple. We may never have another Tall Sequoia, and Tall Sequoia may never win another race.'

Bill shook his head. 'If you had a little sunnier attitude, you could be a pessimist, you know that? He may never win another race, as you say, but he also may win the Triple Crown.'

She sighed. 'Do you know how many horses have won the Triple Crown, my darling?'

'Not offhand. About nine or ten, I guess.' He started to name them, counting on his fingers as he went. 'There was Secretariat, of course, and Seattle Slew and Affirmed. Native Dancer...'

'Nope. Got beat in the Derby by Dark Star.'

39

'Oh, yeah, that's right. Citation, then. I remember now, he was the last before Secretariat. And before that Count Fleet with Johnny Longden, and before that Whirlaway with Arcaro.'

'You forgot Assault in nineteen forty-six.'

'Assault? Are you sure?'

'Positive. Ridden by Warren Mehrtens.'

Bill shook his head. 'If you say so. There were a few in the thirties. War Admiral and a couple more. And the first was—aw, I can't remember.'

'How can you call yourself a horseman, Bill, if you don't live in the past? But I guess you grew up with it. I had to learn this stuff as history, and when you do that you remember it better. The first was Sir Barton in nineteen nineteen. Then Gallant Fox in nineteen thirty, Omaha in 'thirty-five, War Admiral in 'thirty-seven, Whirlaway in 'forty-one, Count Fleet in 'forty-three, Assault in 'forty-six, Citation in 'forty-eight, Secretariat in 'seventy-three, Seattle Slew in 'seventy-seven, and Affirmed in 'seventy-eight.'

'You've got some memory, honey. How many is that?'

'Eleven.'

'So Tall Sequoia will make it a round dozen.'

'That's just a dream, Bill. He can't run with

40

his medicine in New York, can he?'

Bill shrugged. 'We'll cross that bridge when we come to it. It might not hurt him for just one race.'

She rubbed the back of her hand over his cheek. 'Anyway, tell the Mastertons we'll go. It wouldn't be a good thing to miss, I guess.'

'We'll have to pick you out a new dress.'

'No, thanks. No added expenses. They'll have to take me in my overalls or not at all.'

Bill chuckled nervously and hoped she was kidding.

*   *   *

'Well, you'll have to work around me, that's all,' Martin Fine barked into the phone. 'I plan to be in Louisville the whole week of the Derby. There's a big traditional party at Van Ness Masterton's I don't want to miss. And you know having Doc Paul in the race isn't bad publicity for the series. We've been slipping a bit in the ratings. Yeah, yeah, I know we're in no trouble, but if Doc Paul won the Triple Crown it couldn't hurt, right? Also, I can gather some more material for that racing script I want us to do.

'What? Sure, I know I've been on the set for every scene of every episode from day one,

41

and I plan to be again. This is an exception. Hell, no, I'm not losing interest. The day I start to lose interest, the series goes off the air. That's all there is to it. You can work this out. Fred MacMurray used to do a whole season of scenes for *My Three Sons* in a week and a half. You ought to be able to get along without me for a week.'

Soon the conversation ended and the associate producer at the other end of the line, having done his duty in stroking Fine's indispensability myth, briefly gave thanks at the prospect of a whole blissful week on the Dr Paul Ames set without its star in attendance.

★   ★   ★

Bettina Winslow received the engraved invitation from Susie, her black maid and sometime confidante, as she sat lingering over her breakfast coffee. She had to admit it was a classy gesture by Van and his new wife, inviting his most recent ex to join the festivities during Derby week. True, she and Emmett owned one of the top contenders for the race but, even so, they could have been left out quite easily. The Winslow and Masterton farms were close neighbors in Lexington, and there was no reason she should miss the big event. Easy enough to make excuses for Emmy. His nervousness and excessive concern for his charges were well known, and he'd undoubtedly be sleeping in the stall with Pepperpot as Derby day drew nearer, especially with those Old Rosebud letters to jangle his nerves.

'Stand by, Susie, I'll have a reply for you to put in the mail. I don't really want to phone.'

'Written invite, written answer,' the maid said.

Bettina smiled. 'The new Mrs Masterton is a lovely woman, Susie, but I do believe she is a year or two older than I am. That's kind of a surprise, isn't it? You'd expect it to work the other way.'

'The new Mrs Masterton is forty-one. You're going to be forty—'

'Yes, yes, facts at your fingertips as always. I'd say we've both aged well, wouldn't you?'

The maid looked at her appraisingly. 'Your face is a bit more weathered, since you like to take more sun. She's fairer featured, can't take it as well.'

'You have the photographer's harsh eye, Susie,' she said.

'Comes from working in black and white so much,' said the maid. 'Shall I go on?'

'Please do.'

'You have a firmer bust and slightly less

thickening around the middle, but she has better legs.'

'Mine are too skinny. Can't do much about that, can I? Nothing to do with aging. Ah, well. Don't do a physical comparison of Van and Emmett, please. It's not good for me to laugh too hard this early in the morning.'

The maid smiled tightly. Saying exactly what she thought (and what she knew) was one of the things Bettina Winslow paid her for, and she had never yet had the experience of going too far.

'Emmy is so steady and reliable, though. And he gives me more time to myself, wrapped up as he is in his horses. I can't do with more than a part-time husband, Susie.'

As she scribbled her acceptance to the invitation, Bettina reflected that she might very well still be Mrs Van Ness Masterton had it not been for her irritation with the nickname the racing and society press had hung on her: Bat Masterton.

*   *   *

The invitation came to Jerry Brogan's office at Surfside Meadows. As soon as he received it, he was on the phone to Abner Kelley.

'I never expected this. Do they usually invite the media to this thing?'

44

'No, Jerry, though they've been known to ask a selected few. I got an invitation myself, and I wouldn't miss it.'

'It's on Wednesday night, a little earlier than I expected to get to Kentucky. . .'

'Why not come for the whole week?'

'The network will spring for the whole week?'

'They made their stand on your basic fee.'

'Made a stand is right. I got scalped. I'll bet Clem McCarthy never worked for this kind of money, and that was years ago.'

Abner laughed. 'OK, OK! But they told me you were a tough negotiator.'

'Right. A used-car salesman told me that once, too.'

'Anyway, they won't look too hard at your expense account, Jerry. If you play your cards right, you can make up for what you think you lost on your contract. Come on Sunday or Monday and make the Masterton party Wednesday. It's a once-in-a-lifetime opportunity. To some misguided snobs, it's a bigger event than the Derby itself. And the food. . .'

'Are you implying I'd be tempted by the food?' said Jerry, mentally writing his acceptance.

★   ★   ★

Les Randall filed a few lines in the latest article for his London paper about the coming Masterton party.

The Van Ness Masterton party is a Kentucky legend. They say.

The gowns of the ladies put Royal Ascot dowdily in the shade. Or so I am told.

The affair combines the best of Old South hospitality, New South luxury, and general American excess. I reckon.

Masterton's taste and enthusiasm for fast thoroughbreds are matched only by his taste and enthusiasm for beautiful women. Collecting wives of breathtaking features and dimensions—the current Mrs Masterton being the third—does not keep him from surrounding himself with other beauties in abundance. I am assured.

Louisville and Lexington in Derby week are the world capitals of sex and money. By all accounts.

No more must I cock my ear to rumor or hearsay or mere imagination.

For I shall be there.

And so, via this space, will you.

To see how this legendary social event is affected by the churning fear that grips the bluegrass country. To answer questions more vital than who wears what or who beds whom. To wit:

Why do the owners of fancied Kentucky Derby entrants tremble at the name of a nearly forgotten racehorse of the Woodrow Wilson era?

Why do they so fear the name of Old Rosebud?

It was the first time the phantom letter-writer got his name in the paper in any country's press, but it would not be the last.

DERBY 1

The Wednesday evening of Derby week found Jerry Brogan and Abner Kelley proceeding in one of the network's fleet of Oldsmobiles from their Louisville hotel to the Masterton farm outside of Lexington. Ab was driving and Jerry navigating.

'Shouldn't we have dates for this?' Jerry said.

'There should be plenty of interesting ladies there, Jerry,' Ab assured him. 'The bluegrass country is awash with divorcées.'

'The whole world is awash with divorcées, and I'm not really looking for a score. But I wish Donna could have come.'

'Is it the next right?'

'It's quite a way yet. I'll let you know.'
Jerry had visited the farm earlier in the week
to look at the breeding operation and
truthfully had enjoyed that more than he
expected to enjoy the party. Tonight, the
society would be human, and purely social
occasions without Donna he rarely enjoyed
any more aside from the food.

'What's the Masterton place like?' Ab
asked.

'Very grand, very impressive. I didn't get
inside the house, but they gave me a tour of
the paddocks and the stallion barn.'

'They do tours?'

'For people in the business they do. They
used to give a look-around to any tourist who
dropped by, but not many of the big farms do
that any more.'

'Getting unfriendly?'

'It's not that really. Just more security-
conscious, partly because of the times and
partly because of the soaring value of
thoroughbred bloodstock. It's a big business,
Ab.' Jerry sighed. 'They sure filled me in on
the economics of breeding. I got the full sales
pitch on all their stud horses even though I
don't have any mares to bring them.'

'Is this the turn?'

'Next one, I think.'

'All these white fences look alike to me,' Ab confided. 'To tell you the truth, the horses do, too.'

Moments later, they turned onto one of the side roads and under a stone archway that proclaimed *Masterton Farm*. They followed a winding, tree-shaded road to an open area in front of the huge house. A number of cars, few in the economy class, were already parked there.

Formal dress seemed out of place on a working horse farm, but formal it would be this evening. Few of the guests got their hands dirty in the earthier aspects of the thoroughbred business, and on occasions like the Masterton party the old plantation lived on.

'It could be worse,' Ab pointed out as they approached the door. 'It could have been a costume party. Come as your favorite jockey. Or, in your case, come as your favorite horse.'

'Very funny,' Jerry assured him.

A black butler with an ante-bellum face and manner let them into the grand entry hall, its walls lined with oil portraits of famous thoroughbreds.

Carol Masterton greeted them in a dazzling white gown. 'Wonderful to see you again, Abner. Your network is doing wonderful things for horse racing, and I must say it's about time. And Jerry Brogan! I've been so anxious to meet you. They talk about your work all over the country. The best since Harry Henson and Fred Caposella, they say.'

Reflecting that things were looking up, Jerry said, 'I'll have to renegotiate my contract.'

'You mean with Surfside Meadows,' Abner Kelley said quickly, 'not with my network, right?'

'Bill Holman tells me he went to college with you two.'

Jerry said, 'That's right, and what's happened to Bill couldn't happen to a nicer guy. If only one of the three of us could be a big success, I'm sorry it couldn't be me.'

'Bill's a terrific person,' Ab chimed in, 'and I, too, resent his success bitterly.'

Carol laughed. 'This could be quite a reunion. Well, come on into the ballroom. I don't know where Van has got to.'

'If I were him, I'd be guarding Gotham City's stall,' said Jerry.

'So would I,' their hostess agreed smilingly. Gotham City had won the Blue Grass Stakes on schedule, this time beating the previous Mrs Masterton's Pepperpot by three lengths. The Holmans' Tall Sequoia had won the less prestigious Derby Trial on Saturday.

50

Carol led them into the even grander ballroom, elaborately decorated with a racing motif.

Jerry murmured to Ab, 'What great things is your network doing for racing aside from picking up the Triple Crown races on radio and TV?'

'Not a darn thing that I know of.'

Liveried servants, seeming to belong either to another century or to a Hollywood casting office, patrolled the ballroom. Surprisingly, since it had been so associated with the Derby that it seemed more a tourist drink than a real horseman's tipple, the mint julep was the refreshment offered in most abundance, though it seemed other things were available on request. The faces around the room were almost all famous in the thoroughbred world, and the effect on Jerry could only be compared to walking in on one of those movie-studio group shots from the forties. For a fleeting instant, he wished he'd brought his autograph book.

Except for Jerry, Abner, TV's Martin Fine and the ubiquitous Englishman, Les Randall, there was little crossover in attendance with the Holmans' party at the Tokyo Armadillo restaurant. The Holmans, themselves, were there, of course, Arleen looking incredibly lovely. That she wore the same gown she had at her own event bothered Jerry not a bit, and he wondered if Randall was frivolous enough to make such a fashion note a part of his report.

Ab excused himself to cut across the room to talk to the Holmans, while Jerry was introduced to his first celebrities of the evening, Emmett and Bettina Winslow. Considering that Mrs Winslow was the former Mrs Masterton, Carol introduced her with remarkably easy cordiality before sailing off to greet another guest. One would have sworn they were old friends. Bettina was a striking brunette who had more of an outdoorsy look than their hostess. She seemed to have a humorous tolerance of the tall, gaunt man on her arm, who didn't seem at home in a tuxedo.

Emmett Winslow said to Jerry, 'I've heard your work out at Surfside. Liked it. About all I liked out there, to tell you the truth.'

'Please, Emmy,' said Bettina lightly. 'Don't be rude about Mr Brogan's part of the country. Personally, I love Hollywood. I don't know where it is exactly, but I love it.'

'Those hard tracks and that smog aren't good for the horses,' Winslow said.

'Most of the tracks have been resurfaced and aren't as fast as they used to be,' Jerry said. 'Somewhat boring, of course, to have horses moving into the eastern time zone, but it is safer. And we had hoped to solve the smog problem in time for the 1984 Olympics, but. . .'

Bettina laughed. Winslow didn't, but Jerry thought he caught a suggestion of humor in the trainer's eyes.

'Emmy's invasions of California haven't always been too successful, Jerry. If they had been, he'd probably like your state a little better. We thought we had the Santa Anita Derby all wrapped up, didn't we, Emmy?'

The trainer growled something deep in his throat, his Adam's apple bobbing comically.

'But then Pepperpot ups and gets beat by one of those Western sprinters, Tall Sequoia,' Bettina went on. 'That was hard to take, wasn't it, Emmy?'

'He ain't run his best yet. He's still learnin' to be a racehorse. You wait and see. Pepperpot could be the best of his generation. We almost took Gotham City in Florida. As for southern California, Mr Brogan, there's a lot of nice folks out there like everywhere but a lot more crazy people than anywhere else, too. I think everything that's wrong with this country starts out there. Like this Old Rosebud business. It started out there, you know. I got my first Old Rosebud letter when I was out there for the Santa Anita race. It's sick and it's stupid.'

'I'll agree with that. Those letters have a lot of people scared.'

'They don't scare me, but they do make me mad.' The trainer was craning his neck and looking around through the mobs of beautiful people in the room. 'Excuse me, Mr Brogan. I got to see some people. I can't stay for the whole shindig tonight. Don't want to leave Pepperpot for that long. Bet drug me along—'

'I never drug you along!' his wife exclaimed good-humoredly. 'I'd have been perfectly happy for him to stay with the horse, but he loves to come to these things, put on his tux and see all the ladies and trade gossip with all his friends. But he also loves to appear reluctant. And disappear early. Don't you, Emmy?'

'Whatever you say, Bet,' the trainer said, and drifted away.

She watched him go and, though it was hard to imagine this brittle, charming, pampered woman marrying for love, Jerry thought there was some real affection in her look. 'He's a very genuine person, Jerry. Very genuine. He does like to come, but he can't abide more than two hours away from horse dung and the smell of hay.'

Jerry asked her, 'What do you think about this Old Rosebud business, Mrs Winslow? You don't seem particularly concerned.'

Bettina laughed. 'I really think it's a publicity stunt. I expect to see ads for the movie any day. For one thing, I don't really see poison pen by computer, do you?'

'I don't know. No reason why anyone shouldn't take advantage of the latest technological advances.'

'Have you seen any of the letters?'

'No, but I've heard one quoted. One that was in the pocket of a man who had a fatal collision with the rocks at Surfside beach.'

'How dramatic,' Bettina said. 'I don't mean to be callous, but we did hear about him, and everyone was sure it was suicide. But if you want actually to see and touch any of the notorious Old Rosebud letters I have quite a collection in my bag.'

'You carry them around with you?' Jerry said incredulously.

'Oh, yes,' said Bettina, as if it were the most natural thing in the world. 'Come on.'

She led Jerry to an area in the hallway that was being used as a makeshift checkroom. One of the flotilla of servants handed her the bag, and she drew out a group of brief messages on cheap computer paper.

'I think these will be valuable some day, don't you? There are so many odd collecting interests around.'

Jerry looked through them with interest.

55

DON'T PUT TOO MUCH PEPPER IN
THE DERBY STEW. IT COULD GIVE
YOU A DEADLY SNEEZE—OLD
ROSEBUD

IF YOU MAKE THE MISTAKE OF
GOING TO KENTUCKY, WATCH FOR
POISON IVY IN YOUR MINT JULEP—
OLD ROSEBUD

FOREGO THE TRIPLE CROWN,
THAT ANCIENT TITLE, OR YOU'LL
FIND I'M ARMED—OLD ROSEBUD

'If I got one of these things,' Jerry said
frankly, 'it would scare the hell out of me.
That last one especially.'

'Really? I don't know. I think somebody's
just having a good time. I think they're kind
of cute actually. The one about Forego seems
to be one of his standards. I know of at least
three other people who've gotten one just like
it.'

'He repeats himself, eh?'

'Well, he has a computer. He just runs off
another copy.'

'There's something interesting about that
last one.'

'What do you mean?'

'The way he's worked in the names of famous horses.'

'Well, there's Forego, but I don't see any others. Except for Old Rosebud himself. I'm told by some people with long grey beards he was a famous horse at one time.'

'At least two of the others may be before your time, too,' Jerry said with extreme charity. 'Armed was a big winner in the forties for Calumet Farm, and Find won a lot of races for Alfred G. Vanderbilt in the fifties. Ancient Title is comparatively recent, but he ran most of his races out west. They all had something in common with both Forego and Old Rosebud.'

'What's that?'

'Well, they all had long careers. And they had those long careers because they couldn't be used in breeding. They were geldings.'

For an instant, Jerry thought he saw a look of shock or fear flash across Bettina's face. 'Is something wrong?' he said.

She recovered quickly. 'No, no. It's just that you shouldn't use an indelicate word like that in front of an innocent Southern belle like me.' The joke was a nice try, but something had hit a nerve. She pushed the group of notes back into her bag and smiling weakly at Jerry guided him back to the ballroom, clutching his arm rather more firmly than would seem necessary. As they re-entered the room, Jerry caught a suspicious glance from Emmett Winslow, who apparently thought they'd been doing something far less innocent. Jerry couldn't blame the trainer for wanting to keep a close watch on his beautiful wife.

Bettina introduced him to Grant Engle, a lean and handsome middle-aged man who looked like a rodeo cowboy but was in fact Jerry's video opposite number, the man who would call the Kentucky Derby on television for Ab Kelley's network.

'Hi, Jerry.' The guy had a voice many men would kill for, straight from the Golden Age of rich-toned announcers. 'This will be your first Derby, won't it?'

'Right. Usually I have to settle for listening to you.'

Engle gave a rumbling, insincere laugh. 'If you need any help, just turn on the TV during the race. How are you this evening, Bat?'

Bettina Winslow said with pain, 'Grant, I gave up a marriage so people would stop calling me Bat.'

After the trio had exchanged a little more smalltalk, Bettina led Grant Engle away, a possessive hand on his arm. Some kind of meaningful look had passed between them. This apparently was the race-caller that Emmett Winslow should really be suspicious of, but the thin frame of the trainer seemed already to have disappeared for the evening, presumably to return to the Pepperpot watch.

Jerry wondered why he'd taken such a dislike to Grant Engle on such short acquaintanceship. There was nothing wrong with having an air of confidence and sounding like James Earl Jones.

Never alone for long, Jerry saw Martin Fine moving his way.

'Jerry,' said the actor, 'I'm just exactly where I was afraid I'd be. Twenty-first on the list! If I don't get in the Derby, my trainer can go back to taking care of his barnful of claimers. I think one of the big trainers, like Fanning or Lukas, would be glad to take on Doc Paul, don't you? And they'd have been able to make sure he won enough money to get a Derby stall, wouldn't they?'

'Relax, Martin.'

'Relax, relax, he says. People have been telling me all my life to relax. Well, there's a lot of relaxed people on welfare.'

'I doubt that,' Jerry said. 'But, look, it's only Wednesday. My hunch is there'll be at least one scratch by Derby time and Doc Paul will be in.'

'You better be right. And that trainer of mine better hope you're right.'

'How's the racing script coming along?'

59

'Oh, great, great.'

'Are you putting a poison-pen writer in it?'

'No, we did a poison-pen writer our first season. Come to think of it, we did a poison-pen writer our second season, but it was totally different.'

'Any more Old Rosebud letters?'

'I throw that crap away as soon as I lay eyes on it, Jerry. It's getting to be a real drag, especially now it's getting on the news and in the papers.'

'We can thank our friend Les Randall for that.'

'Did I hear my name mentioned?' the English journalist's voice trilled.

Jerry wondered how Randall managed to be everywhere anything was going on in American racing this particular year. It was well known that Randall had been the first to break the Old Rosebud business in his articles, and since then a lot of the American papers and TV stations had picked it up. Fortunately (perhaps), it was still widely regarded as a joke and not a genuine threat, though the death of Denny Kilbride gave it somber overtones.

Martin Fine immediately and conveniently spotted someone he wanted to talk to on the other side of the room and shot away. Jerry had hoped merely to pass the time of day with

Randall and drift away, too, but the journalist's patented brand of offensiveness had a peculiar fascination for him.

'So we approach the great Kentucky Derby, a public relations masterwork,' said Les Randall. 'You know, you Yanks have a lot of nerve calling a mile and two furlongs a classic distance.'

'Maybe we should measure it in meters so you'd like it better,' Jerry answered.

'Come, come, old boy, that's not the point. Britain isn't truly metric, either, yet; and I for one am quite emotionally attached to quarts and pounds and feet and all that sort of thing. But ten furlongs is middle distance, the prey of ambitious sprinters if the pace is right. The one real test in your Triple Crown is the Belmont Stakes at a mile and a half. That is a truly classic distance. Of course, you don't even try to breed stayers over here, do you?'

'Look, *Lezzz*,' Jerry retorted. 'I've seen some English races, and they move so slow in the early going it looks like a six-day bicycle race. The guy calling it doesn't have to wake up until after the first mile.' Imitating a British race-caller, Jerry drawled languidly, 'They're un-dah stahtah's aw-duhs—they're awwff,' and finished it with a loud snore. 'If we had no interest in speed, our horses could run two and a half miles, too.'

'We have the odd opinion that the real running should come at the end, and that the race needn't be decided in the first quarter-mile. Another thing, Jerry, in our main three the first one is a real test of speed—one mile. Then they have to go a mile and a half, then a mile and three-quarters. A horse has to be much more versatile to win our three than to win your three.'

'But our three are run in a matter of six weeks. Your three are spread across the calendar.'

'All the more of a test! To win them all, a horse has to stay healthy and sharp over several months, not just six weeks. I'd much rather have a horse who could win the Two Thousand Guineas, Derby and St Leger than one who could win the Kentucky Derby, Preakness and Belmont.' Randall pronounced the English version 'Darby' and gave the second 'Derby' a satirically harsh American pronunciation.

The discussion was interrupted by the evening's first sighting of their host. Van Ness Masterton, mint julep in hand, was circling the room and asking for reassurance his guests were well supplied. Spotting Les and Jerry, he seemed to make a big effort in the direction of media relations.

'You know something?' he confided. 'I hate

mint juleps. It's part of the tradition, though, so I dutifully put them away.'

Randall pantomimed writing on his cuff. 'Favorite's owner denounces mint juleps,' he said portentously. Jerry didn't find it too damn funny, and the sincerity quotient of Masterton's laugh suggested he didn't, either.

'If you guys want something else to drink, though. . .'

'Mustn't think of it,' said Randall. 'Wouldn't drink anything else during Derby week, would you, Jerry?'

'Not unless there's some warm beer available,' Jerry said.

'I regaled my loyal readership with the mint julep recipe publicity people at Churchill give out. Tell me, Van, is that the same formula your people here use?'

'I have no idea,' Masterton assured him.

'Let's see if I can remember it,' Randall rattled on. 'You make a syrup of two cups sugar and two cups water, boil them together for five minutes. You don't stir it. That's important for some reason. Then you let it cool and pour it into a jar of fresh mint, cover it, refrigerate twelve to twenty-four hours and discard the mint. Then you fill your cup with crushed ice, add half a tablespoon of the syrup and two ounces of Kentucky bourbon. Has to be the very best, they say. Which is the best, by the way? I must mention it in my article. Then you frost the cup and stick in a sprig of mint. What you get looks like this.' Randall took a swallow, seemingly less for enjoyment than to prepare his throat for more talk. 'Now, the novelist James M. Cain did his somewhat differently. Did you see the article on him in *Cuisine*?'

'No,' said Jerry, searching his mind for some subject to get them off recipe trading. Masterton, who had already expressed his dislike for juleps, seemed politely bored.

'Cain said you had to use twice as much bourbon in order to keep the glass frosted.'

'That might help,' said Masterton. 'Yes, indeed. I'll ask them about that in the kitchen. Are you folks getting plenty to eat? It's almost game time, you know.'

'Game time?' said Randall. 'We're not expected to huddle round the telly and watch some stultifying American football match, are we?'

'No, no, this is another kind of game. Sort of racing trivia game. It's another tradition. We're steeped in tradition around here, you know. So steeped sometimes it's hard to move around.'

'Tradition is important, though,' said Les Randall. 'I truly enjoy seeing someone make an effort to keep alive the names of the great old horses. Like this chap that's reviving the memory of Old Rosebud—'

'I don't want to talk about that shit, Les,' said Masterton. 'I said all I'm going to say about that idiot when you asked me the other day. It would have been much better if he hadn't gotten any publicity at all. Not that I blame you, you understand. You're just doing your job. I do understand that. But speaking of tradition, Les, what do you think of the tradition that a horse has to run in the fall to get any real recognition? I know your British classics winners hardly ever run on after they win a big one.'

'I wouldn't say that. More lightly raced, of course, generally than your gee-gees, because there are fewer big purses available and fewer distances to travel. I mean, you understand, distances between courses, not *on* the course, eh, Jerry? It's not uncommon for our top horses to nip over to France for a run at Longchamps or somewhere, but that's scarcely any distance, either, by US standards. Even with the Continental races thrown in, though, there aren't as many money-making opportunities for them as your horses have.'

'And the name of the game is money,' Masterton persisted, 'and the real money in thoroughbred racing today, whatever country you happen to be in, is in breeding, isn't it?'

'Yes, I suppose so, as long as there are plenty of sheikhs around. Not an entirely happy situation, however, and many horse people in my country deplore it—not because they dislike sheikhs, though I must confess some of them *do* in fact dislike sheikhs. Pardon me if I redeploy my journalistic fangs for a moment, Van, but have you and Mrs Masterton come to an agreement yet over the racing future of Gotham City?'

'No need to,' said Masterton, still cordial but with a slight edge to his voice. 'I make the decisions for my stable, and I say what I've said all along. He runs in the Triple Crown races, the classics, practically the only races our TV networks cover and the only races most of the American public knows a damn thing about, and then he retires. Period. Our turf writers, who don't know the game like you people do, will go into a plaintive song and dance about not giving the horse a chance to prove his greatness, as if a horse could read the papers. But let me ask you something: if you had a choice between running around oval tracks for another year or living a life of ease and screwing a different chick every night, which one would you choose?'

Randall laughed nervously. 'There's pressure to perform either way. And screwing a different chick every night, as you so colorfully put it, could get to be a burden after a while, don't you think, Jerry?'

'I wouldn't know,' Jerry said. 'Have to try it first.'

'Pity they can't do both, you know,' Les Randall said. 'Come to the farm and service the mares during breeding season, then back to the racecourse for the rest of the year. Ever think of trying that?'

Masterton snorted with laughter. 'You can do it with mares. I had a pregnant five-year-old mare win a Grade I stakes for me a few years ago. But most stallions would be completely unmanageable on the track once they had a taste of the breeding shed. Anyway, it's still all a matter of economics. Ever heard of something called insurance? Can you imagine what the premiums would amount to on a stud worth millions who takes time off from relatively safe breeding engagements at a couple hundred grand a whack to risk his skinny legs on a racetrack for the same amount? As long as the money is in breeding, the way things are is the way things will be. And don't forget Man o' War never ran past his three-year-old year. Neither did Secretariat.'

'They ran in the fall, though,' Jerry had to point out.

'OK, OK,' said Masterton good-naturedly. 'I know this argument by heart. You should talk to my wife. You'd have a lot in common. But I have a personal reason for wanting to be sure about Gotham City. I've been in racing a long time, and I've never developed a really outstanding stud horse. Weird, isn't it? I've had big winners and made a lot of money, but basically my mares have done it for me. For a long time I thought I had rotten luck. Best prospect I ever had was a royally bred two year old who could run like the wind. At that same time, I also had a cheap and unmanageable colt that we wanted to geld. So what happened? I gave the orders, but the guy running the farm for me at the time, an old turkey called Percy Mayo, castrated the wrong horse! My great stud prospect was still winning sprints for me when he was ten years old, because he wasn't good for anything else. Now, if you fellows will excuse me, I have to set up that little game I was talking about.'

And the horseman disappeared into a corridor off the massive ballroom of the house.

Another hour passed, with no hint that Masterton's promised game was going to begin. Jerry wasn't really looking forward to the game, whatever it was. Since the days of Pin the Tail on the Donkey, he'd had an aversion to party games. And once he managed to shake off Les Randall he began to enjoy himself, spending quite a bit of time with Bill and Arleen Holman, both of whom seemed happier than the last time he'd seen them.

'How long have you been in town, Jerry?' Bill asked.

'Since Monday.'

'We haven't seen you,' Arleen said. 'What have you been doing?'

'Oh, the usual bluegrass country pursuits.'

'Croaking at the Derby-week prices, I bet.'

'No, Jerry's on an expense account,' Bill kidded. 'He doesn't have to worry about how much he has to pay for food and drink and lodging.'

'Neither do the owners of Tall Sequoia,' Jerry said. 'Congratulations on the Derby Trial.'

Arleen thanked him and showed him her crossed fingers. 'I'm really starting to think we have a chance, Jerry.'

Jerry was careful to say nothing about Old Rosebud to the Holmans. He didn't mind unsettling strangers, but these were friends.

He also had an interesting chat with the elderly Acton Schoolcraft, who was something of a legend in racing, breeding and banking circles. Schoolcraft introduced him to Horace

Nurock, the Masterton trainer, who managed to talk about Gotham City without revealing his own view on the horse's future career. He also refused to be drawn out on the Old Rosebud business.

Thus the party seemed to be running like a well-oiled machine without its host, and when Jerry set out from the ballroom to explore the first floor of the house more thoroughly he wasn't really playing investigator as would later be suggested, along with less creditable aims. He was looking for a bathroom. There were a couple off the entry hall, of course, but that was at the other end of the ballroom, and the corridors leading to the rest of the house didn't have *No Trespassing* signs on them.

How many rooms did this place have? he wondered. And how many horse paintings were there on the walls, the parade of horseflesh broken up only occasionally by a portrait of a Masterton ancestor?

Then Jerry noticed something that changed him from sightseer and headhunter to curious would-be sleuth.

One of many doors off the corridor was slightly ajar, and through it Jerry saw what appeared to be a shoe. Not a standing shoe, nor an empty shoe. Someone was lying on the floor of the room. He might have run across someone enjoying an illicit assignation—

Bettina Winslow and Grant Engle, say—and he had no desire to burst in on such a scene. But the foot in the shoe wasn't moving. It seemed to be still beyond even sleep.

Jerry pushed open the door and walked in.

It was a large room that could have been a library or a study or a billiard room. What it mostly was, however, was starkly empty. There was a long table against the far wall with a strange assortment of objects lying on it.

And on the floor, lying parallel to the table, was Van Ness Masterton, blood spreading around him, some sort of dagger or letter-opener protruding from his chest.

Even in the moments after he had realized that his dead and probably murdered host was lying there on the floor, Jerry found himself cataloging in his mind the odd group of objects on the table. It may have been merely a form of shock, but he had some vague idea they might prove important. Each object was clearly separated from the others. There was a framed photograph of a naval officer, a brightly colored comic book, a heavy-looking hardbound volume, a picture of a city skyline, a flashlight battery. There was some sort of a fur stole draped over one end of the table. And a banana with some long strands of hair, like a tail, bizarrely attached to it. And several other

71

documents or scraps of paper. And a brassière.

And a blood-soaked millionaire on the floor below, Jerry reminded himself, trying to spur his stunned mind and body into action. Before he stumbled out of the room, wordlessly summoning one of the anachronistic servants to watch the door, he noticed one more thing. All the red on Masterton's chest was not blood.

There was also a wilted and dying rose.

DERBY 2

The news of Van Masterton's death raced through the ballroom and soon the gathered beautiful people were standing or sitting around in stunned silence, waiting for the representatives of the Lexington Police Department to arrive on the scene. Carol Masterton, on the verge of hysterics, wanted to go to the body, but Jerry restrained her. He knew no one else should be allowed to enter the murder room, and what good could come of it anyway?

In his mind was a jumble of thoughts. He didn't want to tell anyone about the red rose on Masterton's chest. Who knew what kind of panic might ensue if people thought Old Rosebud was not just a harmless crank but a crazy killer? He mentally ran through what he could remember of the objects on the table, trying to sort out their significance. They must have been part of Masterton's promised party game. But what did they all mean? And did they have anything to do with his death?

The profusion of officers on the scene reminded him of an earlier brush with murder back in Surfside. The procedures and the people involved seemed different only in accent. He really wanted to talk to someone at length, but he was asked for his story in bits and pieces first by a uniformed patrolman and finally by the man in charge, a dapperly dressed, rumpled-faced detective named Morton. The principal cop seemed to speak two languages—soft-spoken and courtly to the fragile and important guests, harsh and barking to his subordinates.

Jerry wondered if Morton knew Wilmer Friend of Surfside. It seemed improbable, though. Chiefs of police separated by so many miles of America might be acquainted via conventions, but front-line investigative officers were less likely to be. He really wanted a closer look at the murder room. But what could he say? 'I'm well known as an amateur sleuth out on the coast, don't y'know, and I want to help out with your investigation'? Even if the statement were completely truthful, he wouldn't expect this no-nonsense (and probably extremely competent) detective to suffer a would-be Lord Peter Wimsey gladly. Maybe he should have given himself an extra minute or two in the room before he reported the crime, but at that point he'd been frankly anxious to get out of there.

Deciding to play the role of witness straight, Jerry told Morton the story of how he'd found the body while looking for the bathroom, and that seemed to be all the cop wanted to hear at the moment. Jerry then was told to wait—as universal an occupation at a murder scene as in an army camp.

He moved into a corner, trying to be as invisible as a man of his bulk could manage, and was studying the other people in the room, looking for bloodstains or rose petals or odd expressions or some other clue, when Martin Fine came over to him.

'Jeez, Jerry, they're gonna suspect me of this,' the actor said.

'Why?'

'You remember when I told you what a good story it'd be if the owner of the favorite for the Kentucky Derby was murdered so they'd scratch the horse so the number twenty-one owner could get his horse in? Well, I told that story to a lot of people, Jerry, including some of the best TV writers in the business, and here I am number twenty-one and there's Van Masterton dead. I didn't kill him, Jerry. Believe me.'

'I believe you, Martin,' Jerry said tiredly.

'But aren't they likely to think I did it?'

'I doubt it. For one thing, I don't seriously think Gotham City is going to be scratched from the Derby.' It seemed bad taste even to be talking about it now with the colt's presumed new owner, Carol Masterton, in a state of collapse. 'Anyway, don't conceal anything from them.'

'Oh, I know better than that. I'll tell them all about my script idea first thing. Maybe I can get some pointers for the show. I've never been mixed up in anything like this before. Maybe one of these guys would like to be a technical advisor. You think so?'

'Probably.' Everybody wanted to be a technical advisor, Jerry knew very well. On movies or TV shows or in murder investigations.

It was only after several more hours of waiting, with the police technicians coming and going in bewildering profusion, after the body had been carried out, and numerous others of the guests—presumably the ones

75

with the most money and clout—already interviewed and released, that Morton had Jerry brought into the room where the body had been discovered and asked him the question he'd been waiting half the evening for.

'Mr Brogan, do you have any ideas about this stuff on the table? Nobody seems to know what it all means. Mrs Masterton or anybody.'

Jerry looked at the eleven objects, all carefully separated on the table, just as they had been when he entered the room the first time. He still had a gut feeling they might be important and he was glad for the chance to study them more closely.

A brochure about the United Nations.

A photograph of a man in a naval officer's uniform.

An airplane ticket.

A *Batman* comic book.

A parking ticket.

A picture of a city skyline.

A book on comparative naval strengths of world powers.

A flashlight battery.

A fur stole.

A banana with a few long strands of hair pinned to it.

A brassière.

'You've asked everybody else this?' Jerry

asked. 'And nobody knew?'

'I want to know if *you* know, Mr Brogan.'

'Then, you already know?'

'I didn't say that.'

'Then, nobody knew? Masterton gathered all this stuff and worked out the whole game by himself?'

'What game, Mr Brogan? What do you know about this stuff? Come on. Give us a break.'

'I do have a slight notion,' Jerry said. 'Eleven objects on the table. That's a significant number.'

'What's significant about it?'

'Somebody from the bluegrass country should know.'

For some reason, Morton exploded at that. He was tired and working on a shorter fuse than Jerry had suspected. Suddenly, he was talking to Jerry less as he would to a guest than as he would to one of his subordinates. 'Brogan, I don't like your attitude. I know you're a West Coast hotshot of some sort, but I don't think you're Sherlock Holmes.'

Jerry cringed. That last remark struck a little close to home. 'Sorry. What I meant was, you'd expect somebody who lives here in horse country—'

'I don't see where all this crap has any significance to Kentucky or bluegrass or any damn thing. And you want to know something? I don't even like horses. I'm allergic to horses. And I don't know a damned thing *about* horses. And you know what? There's plenty of people in Lexington and Louisville and all over the state of Kentucky that don't know any bleepin' thing about horses or whiskey or family feuds or bluegrass music or anything else *you* might associate with Kentucky and do just fine. Now, if you got something to tell me, tell me.'

Jerry started to reach for one of the objects. Morton clamped a hand on his wrist. 'Don't touch. Just look. You can see 'em fine.'

'All right. Sorry. Where is that plane ticket to?'

'Omaha, Nebraska. From Louisville. Only thing on that table that has anything about Kentucky. So? What's that mean?'

'Do you know who that's a picture of? The naval officer?'

'Admiral Halsey, I think. Big hero in World War II. My uncle served under him.'

'How about the photo of the city? With the big Space Needle in the middle of it?'

'Seattle. So what?'

'These things seem unrelated, but there's a connection.'

'What connection? Water maybe? Seattle's a major port, and we got a book here on world

78

navies and a picture of an admiral—'

'But Omaha's not a seaport, is it?' Jerry said. 'Unless the Missouri river . . .'

'You were talking about games a minute ago. Well, I think you're playing games with me, Brogan. Out with it. What do all these things mean?'

Jerry looked at them again, thoughtfully. 'It doesn't quite work, though. Almost . . .'

'Look, you're goin' into your Ellery Queen act again. I don't expect a full explanation of everything. Just give me an idea what's in your mind.'

'OK. There's a series of races they call the Triple Crown. That's the Kentucky Derby, Preakness—'

'I know what the Triple Crown is!'

'But you said you didn't know anything about horses.'

'I don't know anything about politics, either, but I know who the governor is.'

'OK. We have eleven objects here. In the history of the Triple Crown, there have been eleven horses who have won all three. Masterton told some of us early in the evening he was planning some kind of game—a party game or a trivia game or something. It was traditional at these parties, and I'm surprised nobody mentioned it to you. What I think he did was to lay out eleven objects, each one representing a winner of the Triple Crown. He was going to challenge the guests to indentify them. I've got most of them figured out, but. . .'

Morton seemed to be losing interest. 'You mean I brought you in here so you could play a guessing game? All these things have no real connection to the death of Masterton?'

'I don't know about that. But look. The ticket to Omaha would point to the nineteen thirty-five Triple Crown winner, Omaha. The picture of Halsey suggests the nineteen thirty-seven winner, War Admiral. What kind of fur is that?'

'Fox.'

'OK, that's a clue to the nineteen thirty winner, Gallant Fox. The guide to the UN points to the nineteen seventy-three winner, Secretariat.'

Morton snorted. 'Silly bastard!'

Jerry grinned. 'Do you mean me or Masterton? No, please don't answer that. The skyline of Seattle points to the nineteen seventy-seven winner, Seattle Slew. The flashlight battery . . . now that's a funny one. It's a pun. Assault and battery. The nineteen forty-six winner, Assault.'

'Oh, brother,' the detective muttered.

'The next one's even crazier. The banana with a tail pinned on it. The jockey who won the Triple Crown in nineteen forty-one, Eddie Arcaro, was known as "Banana-nose", and his mount, Whirlaway, was known as 'Mr Longtail'. Thus, a the banana with a tail. Let's see now. That leaves the book on naval strengths. Count Fleet, the nineteen forty-three winner. And, of course, the traffic ticket points to the nineteen forty-eight winner, Citation.' Jerry was puzzled. 'That leaves the bra and the comic book. But I don't see. . . Yes, I do! There's one missing.'

At that, Morton pricked up his ears. 'One missing?'

'Yes, there should be twelve.'

'You said there were eleven Triple Crown winners. So why should there be twelve objects?'

'Masterton was having fun. He was anticipating a twelfth. His colt, Gotham City, the favorite for the Derby and the most likely of this year's crop to win the Triple Crown. And, as we all know, Gotham City is the place where Batman does his crime fighting and rope swinging. Hence, the comic book.'

Morton nodded his head slowly. 'Sure, I remember. Stupidest damn show in the history of TV. What about the bra?'

'I'm not sure. It must represent either Sir Barton or Affirmed. . .'

The detective gave a grudging chuckle.

'Must be Affirmed.'

'Brassières don't really do any firming, though. It seems far-fetched.'

'Far-fetched? What about Assault and battery?'

'I'd be interested in the brand of the bra.'

'Why?'

'Maybe it's a Maidenform. Sir Barton had never won a race before when he took the first leg of the Triple Crown, the Kentucky Derby. In racing parlance, that made him a maiden.'

Morton peered at the label. 'You got it. Maidenform.'

'There should have been another item here, a twelfth one, that referred to Affirmed. But where is it? Maybe Masterton didn't have it laid out yet. Was there anything else in the room with him? Or on his body?'

Morton looked at Jerry sharply. He hadn't really meant to take the race-caller in as a co-investigator, but it seemed to be happening in spite of him. 'I can't tell you *everything* we know, Brogan.'

'Hey, I'll level with you,' Jerry said. 'I saw the flower on his chest. And I'm sure you must have connected that with Old Rosebud.'

Morton shook his head, as if to clear it. 'Old Rosebud? Is that another horse . . . ?'

'Yes, but didn't anybody tell you about the Old Rosebud letters?'

'No,' said the detective simply. 'What the holy hell are the Old Rosebud letters?'

'I wonder why nobody mentioned it. I'd have thought it would have occurred to everybody first thing. But didn't you tell anybody about the rose on his chest?'

'No, we don't normally tell everybody every damn thing there is to know in a murder investigation, Brogan. It kind of cramps our style. But I can see I should have talked to you first, more than I did. Hey, *you* didn't mention that rose to anybody, did you?'

'No, I didn't think it was a good idea.'

'The servant might have seen it, though. I'll have to get him before... Brogan, it's very important you don't tell anybody about that rose. If we've got some kind of nutty series killer here, we need to know something to separate the real killings from the copycat jobs. God help us if it comes to that, though. Now, what can you tell me about these Old Rosebud letters?'

After telling Morton what little he knew about the turf world's poison-pen writer, Jerry said, 'Old Rosebud was no Triple Crown winner, so that rose wasn't part of Masterton's game. The killer provided that. I suppose he either *is* Old Rosebud or would like to pin his crime on Old Rosebud. And maybe he took the other item with him, the one that was

83

supposed to indicate Affirmed. Why would he do that? Something incriminating?'

'I don't know,' Morton said. He emitted a weary sigh. 'I'd like this to be a nice, simple case. It isn't enough I have to deal with these bluebloods who know everybody from the police commissioner on down. You know, Brogan, cases involving horse people in this town tend to be bad news. You always have to watch your step with the rich and powerful. But that's not enough to deal with. I have to get something out of an old detective novel. Let me get to something a little easier for my poor policeman's brain to understand. Did you see anybody enter or leave this room at the time you were looking for the can?'

'No, I'm afraid not.'

'Nobody saw anything and nobody seems to alibi anybody completely. Somebody came into this room, killed Masterton and slipped out again, and nobody saw him. Or her. When I ask about motive, all I get is what a great guy he was. I understand he had some disagreement with his wife about their horses, but she seemed really broken up about the whole thing. That TV actor seemed nervous as shit...'

'He's like that all the time,' Jerry assured him.

'Masterton's ex-wife's here, and she seemed

pretty hard hit by it, too.'

Maybe for a different reason, Jerry reflected silently. Something about that one Old Rosebud note had scared the hell out of her retroactively. But what?

'Well, I guess you can go, Mr Brogan,' Morton said, returning to the soft tones in which he addressed the guests. 'Sorry if I got a little wrought up there for a while, but this is looking like one bitch of a case. You're staying in town?'

'In Louisville. I expect to be here through Saturday. I'll be flying back to LA on Sunday.'

Morton nodded. 'You gave our people the name of your hotel?'

'Sure.'

'Better give an address we can reach you back home, too. Just in case.'

'There's one other thing you should know,' Jerry added. 'There was a death out in California a few weeks ago that might have been connected with the Old Rosebud murder. A trainer named Denny Kilbride. If you talk to Lieutenant Wilmer Friend of the Surfside police, he can fill you in.'

Morton scowled at the news.

As Jerry left, he reflected that he had now provided two police officers with a mutual headache. And he wondered if by any chance there had been a rose in the vicinity of Denny Kilbride's body.

DERBY 3

In contrast to Martin Fine's scenario, there was never a suggestion that Gotham City would not start in the Kentucky Derby on Saturday, nor was there any question of Carol Masterton's ownership of the colt. There was one defection from the race on Thursday morning, however, when a well-regarded Florida colt named Rapscallion came down with a cough, allowing Doc Paul to join the hunt.

Jerry Brogan spent the last two days before the big race soaking up as much data as he could about the Derby and its current entrants. He spent hours poring over old volumes of turf lore in the library at Lexington's Keeneland racecourse, a sporting maverick Jerry could almost forgive for its years of refusing to employ a public-address announcer. For current information, he stalked the backstretch of the historic Louisville track. He made all the press conferences and didn't miss a moment of media hype (or one free meal) preceding the big race.

Whichever of the score of three-year-old colts (and one filly) got there in front on Saturday, he was determined to have something unusual to report. He tried to find out what each entry liked for breakfast. (To his disappointment, it was oats mostly, not a beer drinker or chocolate-éclair eater in the lot.) He researched the background of the owners and trainers and jockeys, knowing who had been here before and when and also how they had done. He wouldn't use all this, but would have it at his fingertips if needed. He knew or found out how long it had been since the big race had been won by a gray (Gato Del Sol, 1982) or a filly (Genuine Risk, 1980) or a gelding (Clyde Van Dusen, 1929) or a California-bred (Decidedly, 1962) or a Canadian-bred (Sunny's Halo, 1983) or a horse foaled outside North America (the English-bred Tomy Lee, 1959). While Pepperpot had been bred and raised at one of the largest thoroughbred farms in the world, Tall Sequoia was the product of one of five mares who lived on Bill and Arleen Holman's three-acre property in California. Questing Willie, the late Denny Kilbride's hopeful, had been sold as a yearling for a mere $5000, and Valid Point had brought half a million at the Keeneland yearling sales.

In the midst of his research, Jerry could never put the mystery of Van Ness Masterton's death completely out of his mind, and of course he kept seeing fellow attendees at the Masterton party as the week went on. As subtly as he could, he continued to do an informal survey of the Old Rosebud letters. The anonymous letter-writer was common coin now, both in the media and in casual conversation, but since the rose on Masterton's chest had not been revealed publicly the extent of the possible connection was not known, only rumored.

Jerry was disappointed that he never heard from Morton on Thursday. He had somehow expected to be kept abreast of what was happening in the investigation. At one point on Friday morning he had what he thought was a helpful suggestion and called the detective at headquarters.

'Do you have anything on the missing item yet?' Jerry asked.

'Missing item? Oh, yes, the party game thing. No, and I have to tell you we haven't pursued that angle very hard once we established that nobody helped Masterton work out the game. Understand, we don't throw out anything that might be useful, but that doesn't seem to me to be one of the most important things.'

'Well, I have an idea about that. I've been trying to think what I might use to designate Affirmed in that game Masterton was planning. Now, where do you usually hear or see that word "affirmed"?'

'No guessing games, Mr Brogan. I don't have time. You tell me.'

'On a Supreme Court decision, or a ruling handed down by some other appellate court. They normally either affirm or reverse the decision of the lower court. Now, suppose Masterton had laid out a copy of a court decision to represent Affirmed. And suppose that court decision had some particular meaning to the person who killed Masterton. Maybe it would provide some kind of link between the killer and Masterton, point to a possible motive. Thus, the killer grabbed it and took it with him. Or her. You didn't search us.'

'No reason to. We had the weapon, after all. And to start doing searches on all the people at that party I'd need a good reason, believe me.'

'What have you found out about the weapon, by the way?'

Morton sighed. 'No harm in telling you, I guess. It was a cheap, ordinary letter-opener. It might have been there on the premises or it might have been brought by the killer. We don't even know that. We considered the possibility that it might have been the twelfth item on the table, assuming there were supposed to be twelve as you say.'

'No connection with Affirmed, though.'

'No, not really. Of course, I'm not personally acquainted with the horse. Does he open his own mail?'

'Fingerprints?'

'Nothing usable, no. No hoofprints, either. Well, this is all very interesting, Mr Brogan, about the court decision, but it's just guesswork and I don't know what you want me to do with it. If there was such a court report, and the killer left the Masterton house with it, it's probably been destroyed by now.'

'That copy of it's been destroyed, but the report still exists somewhere. Maybe you could find out if Masterton or any of the guests have been involved in an appellate court decision. If we find that decision, we may have a key to the motive for Masterton's murder.'

'Mr Brogan,' said Morton with a tone of strained patience, 'that sounds like it would take a powerful lot of time, and our computer really isn't programmed to do that kind of a search. If there is such a case, we wouldn't even know what jurisdiction it was decided in.'

'Well, you could start with Kentucky, then

maybe go to the US Supreme Court and the district federal courts, then try some of the other major racing and breeding states, like California, Florida, Maryland, Virginia, New York. . .'

'I'll tell you, Mr Brogan, if you want to do that and report the results to us, we'll be more than happy to have a look at them. This is one instance where we would welcome a little amateur detective work. Now, you just call me and tell me what you find out.'

Bristling at the detective's patronizing tone, Jerry made his goodbye briefly and hung up the phone. That's what he got for trying to help. True, it would be a needle-in-a-haystack operation. But still, if you assumed the case had to do with racing or breeding, how many such cases got reported in the various law reports? It might not be that overwhelming a job. But from the standpoint of practical police work he could see why Morton was dubious.

After a long-distance call to a law-librarian friend in California, Jerry put amateur detection aside and left his hotel room for yet another press event.

★　　★　　★

There were three people seated at the table in

the Louisville restaurant to meet the media that Friday morning, not more than thirty-six hours after the death of Van Ness Masterton. Carol Masterton, Horace Nurock and Acton Schoolcraft. And the media, print and broadcast, were there in force.

Carol, looking subdued but quite beautiful, read a statement about her determination to continue the Masterton thoroughbred tradition. Since Masterton had died without children, the whole operation now belonged to her. She stated her gratitude to the great trainer Horace Nurock and trusted advisor Acton Schoolcraft in helping her through a difficult couple of days. She reiterated that Gotham City would indeed start in the Kentucky Derby as planned, as a memorial to her husband.

Following her statement, the questions from reporters began.

'What are the plans for Gotham City after the Triple Crown races, Mrs Masterton?'

Carol licked her lips and looked to the two men on either side of her. 'We've scarcely discussed that ...'

Acton Schoolcraft spoke. 'It had been tentatively planned by Van Ness Masterton that the colt would be syndicated following the Triple Crown events. However, if this course still is followed, the possibility exists of further racing depending upon the desires of Mrs Masterton and the members of whatever syndicate might be formed.'

'What's your opinion, Mr Nurock?'

'Well,' the trainer said with a slight smile, 'I look at it from a prejudiced point of view. As a trainer, I like to see great horses stay on the racetrack, especially ones in my barn. However, I naturally will go along with whatever decision Mrs Masterton chooses to make.'

'Isn't it true, Mrs Masterton, that the idea of racing Gotham City later in the year represents a break with your husband's wishes?'

She replied, 'As Mr Schoolcraft has said, no definite decision has been made as yet. Only a day has passed since . . .'

As she controlled herself with an effort, the media bore on relentlessly. 'Mrs Masterton, do you have any idea who murdered your husband?'

'No, I do not,' she said. 'But I'm confident and hopeful the killer will be brought to justice.'

'Any connection with these Old Rosebud letters we've been hearing about?'

'I know nothing about Old Rosebud letters.'

'What about you, Mr Nurock? Did you or

Mr Masterton receive any of these letters?'

'Everybody did, as far as I can tell,' said Horace Nurock. 'We all figured it was just a crank, and that's still what I think. I don't see any connection with the death of Mr Masterton.'

'Do you have any of the letters with you?'

A publicity representative of Churchill Downs jumped in at that point. 'All of these letters that have been kept by their recipients have been turned over to the police. And any questions regarding that crime should be directed to the proper police authorities in Lexington.' Not a Louisville matter, he seemed to imply.

Then one of the reporters actually seemed to take the admonition to heart and asked Nurock a question about the condition of Gotham City and how he was coming up to the Derby. The relieved trainer answered in greater than usual detail. Shortly thereafter the press conference broke up. Jerry, standing at the back of the room, though as intrigued as anyone, wondered about the taste of the morning's entertainment.

★   ★   ★

Sometime after four o'clock the following day, Jerry was sitting in the broadcast-booth above the Churchill Downs fifth-floor pressbox, his binoculars trained on the twenty horses going to the post for the Kentucky Derby. The traditional playing of 'My Old Kentucky Home' did not bring him to the brink of tears; indeed, he hardly heard it. Memorizing a field this large was a new experience for him. The most that had ever gone postward together at Surfside Meadows was fifteen, and that had been considered a cavalry charge. The five minutes before the Derby he would have to spend talking to his radio audience, so he had to be sure he had all the colors and other identifying details committed to memory by then.

The tote board showed that Gotham City was favorite at 9–5. They seemed generous odds for an undefeated colt who some felt was a world beater, especially a beautiful chestnut with picture-perfect conformation, but the bettors knew anything could happen in the Kentucky Derby, especially with an overflow field in the gate. Tall Sequoia, a spotted roan with a reddish tinge to his glossy coat, was second choice at 3–1; while Bettina and Emmett Winslow's Pepperpot, a rather ordinary-looking bay who had been something of a trial horse for both of the top two, was held at 7–2. The odds on Martin Fine's coal-black Doc Paul was 12–1, a somewhat shorter price than might have been expected for the twentieth-best earner. The owner, of course, had been receiving more than his share of pre-race publicity until the Masterton murder had somewhat redirected the media's focus. There was a filly, Lescania, held at 15–1 in her bid to join Regret (1915) and Genuine Risk as female Derby winners.

The flash from western Canada, Penticton, was offered at what Jerry thought was a generous price of 20–1. The Arkansas and Louisiana Derby winner Valid Point also seemed something of a bargain at 10–1. Another Californian, Questing Willie, who had been co-owned and trained by the ill-fated Denny Kilbride and now raced in the colors of his surviving partner (no Kilbride heir having been found), was thought even by Westerners to be a pure sprinter and was offered at 50–1. The extreme longshot at 60–1 was a colt from Washington State called Brave Invader. Sounds like a classic-winner anyway, Jerry reflected. On form, these last two probably should have been 99–1, the longest odds that could be shown on the tote board, which really meant the sky was the limit. But this was the Kentucky Derby, and the public would seldom let a horse go off at such long odds, especially in a field of twenty. No less than nine horses were linked together in the mutual field and, as often happened in the Derby, that bargain-basement betting interest had been backed way down. Nine for the price of one was hard to resist, and the long-memoried fans may have remembered Canonero II, a field-horse winner in 1971, or Count Turf twenty years earlier. The group of nine were now 6–1 fourth choice.

From Jerry's quiet survey, it seemed that virtually no owner with a Derby hopeful had escaped receiving at least one Old Rosebud letter, but even after the death of Van Ness Masterton it didn't seem to be scaring any of them off.

With only moments to go to air time, Jerry panned his glasses around at the crowd. The infield was packed with people who would never even see the race, or much of it. But they had a great view of the tulip beds, another Kentucky Derby tradition. Unlike most newer racetracks, Churchill Downs was located in the heart of the city, and Jerry could see the traffic moving on Longfield Avenue beyond the backstretch area.

The tote board flashed. Jerry noted some sudden action on Penticton, who dropped to 15–1, while Doc Paul's price edged up to 14–1. Most of the others stayed constant.

The engineer's signal told him he was on the air. Clutching the mike with white-knuckled fingers, Jerry looked as nervous as he felt.

'Good afternoon from Louisville, Kentucky. This is Jerry Brogan speaking, and we are moments away from the running of the Kentucky Derby. A field of twenty will go to the post under the shadow of the Churchill Downs spires. An estimated hundred and twenty thousand people have jammed the infield and the old grandstand, which breathes history through every board. They've come to see which runner will prevail down the long, long stretch this afternoon. Will it be the favored Gotham City, whose owner Van Ness Masterton died tragically only days before the race? Or will it be Valid Point, who seems to run his best in state Derbies, having prevailed in the Louisiana and Arkansas Derbies already? Then there is Bettina and Emmett Winslow's Pepperpot, who has been a perpetual second-place horse in the top three-year-old stakes. Or will it be a member of the strong California contingent, led by Tall Sequoia, an impressive Santa Anita Derby winner from the stable of Bill and Arleen Holman, and Doc Paul, named for the character owner Martin Fine plays on a popular television series?'

★　　　★　　　★

Donna Melendez, sitting by her radio back in California, was noticing how smooth and relaxed Jerry sounded. He was talking fairly fast, having prepared plenty about each entrant and wanting to get it all in, but she didn't have the drama teacher's impulse to implore him to slow down. His voice held just the right edge of excitement. The words poured out until two minutes to post, when he broke for a commercial. Donna had switched on the TV picture of the race while listening loyally to Jerry's radio call. She wished she could have gone back as he'd invited, but the spring play was into Saturday-morning rehearsals now.

*   *   *

Jerry realized he was sweating and mopped his wet brow with the back of his hand. Talking his way through the program and his copious notes was the easy part. Calling the actual race and getting it right would be the tough part.

The horses were now loading into the gate at the head of the stretch. What a feat it would be to get twenty of them ready to go at once. The race-caller may have a tough job, but what about the starter and his crew? Some of the assistants sat in the stall with the horses, holding their bridles before the start. Dangerous work.

The radio network came perilously close to missing the start. Two seconds after the engineer gave Jerry his finger cue, the gates flew open and Jerry proclaimed, 'They're off!'

★   ★   ★

Donna wanted to close her eyes when she saw the cavalry charge of twenty burst from the gate. There seemed to be so much bumping and lurching going on, she didn't see how the jockeys could manage to stay on, let alone get their horses in good position. Just let them all get around safely, she prayed.

It amazed her Jerry was calling the names of horses. How did he manage to sort them all out? He was good at his job.

'Questing Willie goes for the lead. Mop Away is second. Tall Sequoia is third. Then it's Lescania.'

★   ★   ★

The first run through the long Churchill Downs stretch belonged to the sprinters. The lightning-fast Questing Willie had broken like a quarter horse, but soon he was joined in the lead by a field horse, Mop Away, who had earned enough to get into the race on the basis of winning a rich Arizona futurity. They were running so fast, it seemed certain they would burn each other out long before the finish. Concentrating on reeling off the names of all twenty runners, Jerry fleetingly thought the jockey on his old friend's Tall Sequoia might be ruining the roan colt's chances of staying so close to the pace. And he thought another Californian, Doc Paul, had lost a couple of lengths at the start.

As the field went into the first turn, the first four remained the same, with the bulk of the field in one large bunch, like a swarm of bees. Jerry watched Doc Paul go some eight horses wide on the clubhouse turn. This did not seem to be the hope of Hollywood's lucky day. Astonishingly, though, the favorite was not doing much better. Gotham City was a couple of lengths behind the main pack, with only a pair of field horses behind him. The Masterton horse, who customarily ran much closer than that to the pace, must also have been pinched back at the start.

Jerry glanced at the tote board and reported to his listeners that the first quarter had been run in less than twenty-three seconds, much too fast for a Kentucky Derby start if the leaders expected to be around at the finish.

As the field entered the backstretch,

Questing Willie was already beginning his quest for the rear of the pack. Mop Away, though, was hanging firm, holding the lead on the rail with Tall Sequoia about a half-length behind him. Another length farther back, the filly Lescania was holding third. Pepperpot and Valid Point were asserting themselves, emerging from the pack side by side. Penticton and Brave Invader seemed well placed, but both Doc Paul and Gotham City were still far back.

'The half was run in forty-six and one. Approaching the far turn, it's now Tall Sequoia showing in front on the outside by a neck. Mop Away is second but beginning to weaken. Valid Point is now third between horses, moving to challenge the first two. Lescania is fourth by a head; Pepperpot is now fifth along the rail; the rest are well bunched. Penticton is sixth; Rocking Wagon is seventh; Brave Invader is eighth; Questing Willie is ninth; Fortuitous is tenth, followed by... He ran through all the rest of the names, finding Gotham City in sixteenth, beginning a tepid move, and Doc Paul in seventeenth. And that was the last time most of these steeds would get their names on the radio today.

The horses made the turn for home. Amazingly, the field seemed to get tighter instead of more strung out. Tall Sequoia held a short lead, with Valid Point and Pepperpot both challenging. Mop Away had carried his considerable speed and heart as far as he could and was falling back. The jockey on Lescania had already gone to the whip, suggesting she would also be backing up before long. The rider on Gotham City had managed a broken-field run to get his colt into fifth place and contention.

'Into the Churchill Downs stretch, it's Tall Sequoia, gamely holding a neck lead; Pepperpot is now second on the outside by a half-length; Valid Point is third between those; Gotham City now moves up to fourth on the outside and making a powerful move. It's not far back to Penticton in fifth; Rocking Wagon, still in the hunt, is sixth. And here comes Doc Paul, moving fast out in the middle of the track!'

Jerry couldn't believe what he was seeing. There seemed to be seven or eight of them in a tight group in the Churchill Downs stretch, all running hard, nobody giving up. For an instant an eighth of a mile from home the favored Gotham City got his head in front for a brief lead. But he began to hang and the Canadian colt, Penticton, thrust his nose into the vanguard. Tall Sequoia, far from quitting, seemed to be coming on again. Pepperpot, head down, forged on determinedly. Doc Paul was moving fastest of all on the outside. All the jockeys pumped furiously, most going to the whip. The whole group flashed under the wire together, and Jerry did his best to bring order from chaos.

'Pepperpot wins the Run for the Roses by a nose! Penticton is second by another nose with Doc Paul third by a half a length and Tall Sequoia fourth, followed by the favored Gotham City, Rocking Wagon and Valid Point. This may have been the closest blanket finish in the history of the Kentucky Derby, but as I saw it from here Pepperpot, a perpetual runner-up in many of the major stepping stones, got the call, barely beating out Penticton, the pride of British Columbia. The photo-finish sign has, of course, gone up, and we'll have the official result for you momentarily. We'll be back after this message.'

★　　★　　★

Donna thought the race had been dazzling. And so had Jerry's call. How could he possibly tell which of those charging thoroughbreds had won? While a commercial poured out of the radio, the TV camera was following one of the horses running back toward the front side and, presumably, the winner's circle.

But suddenly Donna realized it wasn't the same horse Jerry had called the winner. The graphic on the screen said, 'Penticton, Kentucky Derby winner.'

*　　　*　　　*

Jerry slumped back in his chair. The engineer leaned over and whispered, 'The TV guy called Penticton.'

'I don't give a flying fetlock what the TV guy called,' Jerry said with a scowl. The engineer held up his hand for quiet.

Jerry replayed the finish mentally. Their heads had been bobbing at the wire, and any one of three could have got it. But he saw it Pepperpot, and Pepperpot he called it. You had to call a winner, and Jerry seldom missed even the closest of photo finishes. It could easily have been a dead heat, but a race-caller rarely calls a dead heat, almost always goes out on a limb and names a horse.

He watched the replay on the TV monitor in front of him. They froze the videotape right at the wire. Maybe he should have said it was too close to call, but that was a cop-out.

The commercial over, Jerry gabbed on, mentioning the owners, trainers and jockeys of all the colts in the photo finish, throwing in bits of color he had left over from before the race. He even had some material to share on Derby blanket finishes. The last really close one had been in 1969, when Majestic Prince had prevailed by a neck over Arts and Letters and Dike. But only the 1946 running, when Jet Pilot beat Phalanx and Faultless, could approximate this three-horse photo, and even there the margins had been heads rather than noses.

To unsettle things further, the *Inquiry* sign on the tote board began to flash. Presumably, one of the jockeys had claimed foul. A stewards' inquiry would have started the sign flashing immediately after the finish. Jerry hadn't seen anything untoward, unless it happened at that wild start, and it was widely claimed that no winning horse's number would ever come down in the Kentucky Derby, regardless of the rodeo tactics of the riders. In the 1933 running, Don Meade on Broker's Tip and Herb Fisher on Head Play had had a virtual wrestling match en route down the Derby stretch, and no numbers had come down that day. In 1984, Gate Dancer had been disqualified, but from a minor placing, not from the win.

It seemed an eternity until the result of the photo came up. When it did, Jerry saw that he would not be the one to dine on crow. A skinny trainer in Kentucky and a drama teacher in California were also among those heaving sighs of relief.

'The winner of the Kentucky Derby is Pepperpot, owned by Mrs Bettina Winslow and trained by her husband Emmett Winslow. Second was Penticton and third was the fast-closing Doc Paul. Tall Sequoia was fourth. The time was a highly respectable two/o-one flat.'

Then the *Inquiry* sign went off, followed by the unsurprising announcement that there would be no change in the order of finish. The prices came up, and Jerry told his listeners that Pepperpot had paid $10.40 to win, going off at slightly more than 4–1 as the third choice in the wagering.

Jerry wrapped up his broadcast once the prices had come up, then gave his attention to the TV monitor where the post-race interviews were coming on.

Emmet Winslow was saying 'I told everybody this was a colt that wouldn't settle for seconds and thirds forever, but not many folks believed me. Look at him now.'

Bettina Winslow, looking radiantly happy, was tactlessly asked if the sad events of the week took some of the edge off winning the Kentucky Derby.

'Nothing could spoil this moment,' she said. 'It's once in a lifetime.' She was almost convincing. But at one point in the post-race ceremony Jerry thought he detected a flash of the fear she had shown at the Masterton party.

The Governor of Kentucky had presented the winning owners with a sterling-silver julep-cup. Tradition called for the owner of the winner to drink a toast to the victorious horse. Did Bettina seem to hesitate before she drank, or did Jerry just imagine it? At any rate, the winning owner did not drop dead on the spot.

After the race, Jerry dutifully tried to console his television opposite number, Grant Engle.

'We all blow one now and then, Grant,' Jerry said. 'Chic Anderson was great, but he called the wrong horse in the stretch in the Derby a few years ago.'

'He didn't call the wrong horse at the finish.'

'Clem McCarthy once called Jet Pilot the winner of the Preakness, when it was Faultless.'

'He was old and had bad eyes. What's my excuse?'

Engle seemed to enjoy wallowing in misery. Jerry wondered if he would be any less pitiful if he had been the one to call the wrong winner. He hoped so, but it was best not to find out.

*   *   *

The post-Derby news was like most post-Derby news. At least one of the top finishers would skip the Preakness and go home. This time it was Doc Paul, the owner announcing he would return to California. 'I was very, very, very proud of my little horse,' Martin Fine told reporters. 'He would have won easily if he'd been able to get away better at the start and hadn't had to go so wide on the first turn. But we all have to overcome adversity. That's what life is about. That's what my show is about. And we've got some great shows coming up, more hard-hitting than ever.'

At least one Derby colt would opt out of the Preakness with an injury. This time, it was Gotham City. Horace Nurock said the chestnut colt had a quarter crack, a very minor problem, and should be ready in time for the Belmont Stakes. If he'd had a chance to win the Triple Crown, he could have been pointed for the Preakness with what was called a Bane patch on his injury, but under the circumstances there was no reason to take a chance with such a valuable animal. No

109

excuse was offered for his Derby performance though many observers thought his racing luck had been nearly as bad as Doc Paul's.

It still figured to be a good and contentious Preakness. The winner of the Derby, Pepperpot, who would clearly benefit more than the runner-up by the shorter distance of a mile and three-sixteenths, was universally hailed as the logical favorite. Penticton would be there to contest matters with him, as would fourth-place finisher Tall Sequoia. Also coming back from the Derby field were Valid Point, Rocking Wagon, Brave Invader and (surprisingly) the front-running southwesterner Mop Away. The failure of the Derby to produce a standout figured to give hope to several additional Preakness entries not previously heard from, including the late Derby-week scratch, Rapscallion.

★　　★　　★

Greeting Jerry Brogan at the airport, Donna demanded, 'Why don't they let you do the next one on TV? You called the right horse, and the TV guy called the wrong one.'

'I agree that it would be fair to hang the poor guy for one mistake, but who said the world was just? We'll be in our same familiar roles for the Preakness.'

110

One more Derby-week personality would also be in the same familiar role for the Preakness, though the citizens of Baltimore would have been less welcoming had they known: Old Rosebud.

BETWEEN RACES 1

Jerry puffed along the wet sand of Surfside Beach, sure he would drop at any moment, and watched the flashing brown calves leaving him farther and farther behind. Finally Donna had mercy on him and slowed down, giving him a chance to catch up.

'You're letting these beach bunnies distract you, Brogan,' she charged.

Jerry gasped out his injured innocence. 'That's not true. The rear view of your magnificent form is the only thing that's kept me going this far.'

She shook her head. 'You can't fool me. Even if I could kid myself I was Miss America, or better yet Miss Mexico, I don't see how I could compete half-dressed with girls that are for all practical purposes naked.'

Jerry smiled. He knew she had a bikini on under the shorts and sweatshirt. 'I was watching you, but if you think you should compete on an even basis there's no reason why you couldn't. I might increase my speed that way.'

'Sorry,' she said. 'I can't concentrate on my running if I'm afraid of something coming loose.'

'Then, let's concentrate on lying down,' Jerry said, making a bee-line for the towels where they had left them a few yards up the beach. She followed reluctantly.

'You've hardly given me a chance to work up a sweat,' she said.

'Not so. There are four tiny drops below your headband, and it's the most sweat I've seen out of you in the daytime since—'

'OK, OK.' She flopped down on the towel. 'You mind if I delay my striptease? I don't want to catch cold.'

'Sure.' Jerry lay there feeling like a beached whale, trying to get his breath. It was mid-morning on what promised to be a hot day, and Surfside Beach was starting to get crowded. The Kentucky Derby had been run one week before, and the Preakness Stakes, second of the Triple Crown events, would be run at Baltimore's Pimlico racecourse one week later.

'You still seem distracted, Jerry,' Donna said after a few minutes' silence.

'I don't believe it,' he said. 'How can you

112

read my face when it's red as a beet and gasping for air? Besides, I'm only looking at you.'

'I don't mean your taste in sideshows. What are you thinking about?'

'Breathing. Continuing to live.'

'Seriously. Been investigating your murder this week?'

'This one isn't my murder. And no.'

'You haven't been on the phone to Wilmer Friend?'

'Only once. And just to pass along a suggestion. My civic duty.'

'Did he appreciate the suggestion?'

'Not very much. I just asked him if there'd been a rose in the vicinity of Denny Kilbride's body when he went over the cliff.'

'And had there?'

'No. He'd already heard about the Old Rosebud calling card from the Lexington cops. He seemed to think I just went back to Kentucky to create more trouble for him. He still insists Denny's death was an accident or maybe suicide and that he has plenty of real crime to contend with. So the Lexington police can solve their own murder.'

'So you're feeling unappreciated?'

'By no means. Why should I be appreciated anyway? Look, you brought this business up. I haven't even been thinking about it.'

113

'I'm sure not.'

'So what do you want to do this afternoon? It's going to get hot on this beach.'

'What did you have in mind?'

'Lunch.'

'Yeah, I figured lunch. Lunch is usually nice around midday. Where lunch?'

'Remember Bluto's?'

'Bluto's?' She made a face. 'Not my favorite.'

'You liked their spinach salad, remember?'

'I did not.'

'Sure you did. It's their specialty.'

'Specialty or not, I hated it. You did, too. You said it was Bluto's revenge on Popeye. They go 'way too heavy on the vinegar.'

'The substitute chef was on that day.'

'They have chefs? I don't want to go to Bluto's, Brogan.'

'How about the Blue Book?'

'I don't remember the—That's not the place where the menu looks like a college exam booklet, is it?'

'That's why they call it the Blue Book. But you can't judge a restaurant by its menu.'

'What do you want at the university, Jerry?'

'University?' he said innocently.

'You mention two lousy eating places that are practically on the campus. Therefore, the location must be more important to you than

114

the food.'

'I thought we might drop in at the library. If we were in the neighborhood.'

'Jerry, I love libraries, but it's a beautiful spring day and we're not cramming for finals.'

'It won't take long. Just something I want to check on, that's all.'

'Oh, all right, I'll have a look at some of the theater journals while you're checking what you want to check.'

'Uh, I don't think they take those at the law library, Donna.'

'The *law* library? This gets more boring by the minute.' She shed shorts and top with amazing speed and grace and stretched her brown, smooth-muscled body in the sun. That which polite society demanded be covered was, but not a square inch more.

Jerry grinned appreciatively and ran a tickling hand over her belly. But the effect of her misdirection was short-lived. Two hours later, they were in Surfside University's well-stocked law library.

*   *   *

Walt Hinkel, one of the several SU law librarians, was rumored to be independently wealthy. That he had shared ownership in several notably unsuccessful racehorses added fuel to the rumors. But he chose to work at his trade because he wanted something to do, and he really enjoyed the exacting work of tracking down obscure legal references for lawyers and law students. At the moment, he was harried and apologetic.

'I meant to get to it all week, Jerry, but we've been swamped. The law school really has to give us a larger staff.' He glanced over his shoulder at a formidable-looking band of students approaching the reference desk. 'Look, though, I did make a list of possible Digest topics and terms to look up in the Descriptive Word Index. And don't forget to check the pocket parts. So you just take these, and I'll get back to you later, OK?'

'But I've never used . . .' Jerry began.

'It's OK,' Donna assured him. 'I took a class in this once.' She took the lists and led Jerry toward the endless ranges of red- and green-covered Digests. Walt Hinkel relievedly returned to his post.

'I didn't know you knew anything about legal research,' Jerry said admiringly.

'Took a seminar in Women's Legal Rights in college, and they taught us to use all this crap. But we're not taking all day, Brogan. I'm just an educator Monday through Friday. Let's get going.'

They pored over the indexes alone until

four o'clock. Then Walt, freed of pressure from mere students of the law school, joined them. At six, Walt closed the library, which stayed open till midnight every night of the week but Saturday. At seven twenty-nine, one of them found the case Jerry wanted. (Each was inclined to take the credit, so who actually found it was never established for sure.)

Jerry suggested some dinner. Donna expressed enthusiasm. Walt suggested Bluto's. He said they made a great spinach salad.

★   ★   ★

'The case is called *Cranstone Bloodstock Company vs. Hopper*,' Jerry said into the phone Monday morning. 'It was an inter-state thing, so it was decided in a federal district court and went on to a district court of appeals. Masterton himself wasn't a party to the action, but—'

'Why are you telling me this, Jerry?' Wilmer Friend asked. 'It's not my case.'

'I'd suggest an equipment change for your next race, Lieutenant,' Jerry snapped. 'Friend, blinkers off!'

'What are you talking about?' Lieutenant Friend, despite his proximity to the racetrack, had never become a racing fan. 'You're not

117

making sense.'

'I kind of imagined I could pass this information to you and you could pass it along to Lexington. Don't you people co-operate with each other?'

'You wanted to stick us with the phone call, huh? Why don't you call them directly? Won't the track spring for it?'

'I can make whatever phone calls I want. Look, I just wanted to try this out on you first. Is that OK?'

'You want a dry run on the police mentality course, huh? All right, all right, go ahead. And if I think there's anything to it I'll pass it along to Lexington. If I don't, it's better they hear it from you anyway.'

'Cranstone Bloodstock Company held an option on several future breeding seasons to a well-bred colt called Blueskying, owned by Van Ness Masterton.'

'Futures options? Jerry, if anything makes me sicker than racing jargon, it's financial jargon. I don't even like *Wall Street Week...*'

'Just listen, Wilmer. Who's wasting whose time here? The crew at the Masterton farm, who aren't mentioned by name in the case report, were supposed to geld another two year old and gelded Blueskying by mistake. Besides costing Masterton a lot of money,

118

their booboo obviously made any option on breeding seasons worthless. The bloodstock company claimed Masterton had been negligent and tried to get back from Masterton three broodmares they had delivered to him in exchange for the options. Masterton didn't contest it and either returned or made them a settlement on two of the mares, but the third had been provisionally sold to a breeder named Claude Hopper who had her in foal to Secretariat and would not return her to Masterton or to Cranstone Bloodstock or agree to a cash settlement. So Cranstone, in what one of the justices describes as an unusual end run, brought suit against Hopper.'

'I hear there are a lot of old football players on the federal bench. Where is this leading?'

'The Cranstone lawyers pointed to a clause in Hopper's contract with Masterton that seemed to suggest the sale would be off if there was any question of Masterton's own title. Hopper's lawyers said there really wasn't a question about Masterton's title, that he still owned the stallion, even though he was now a gelding. It was an obscure point, Wilmer, but as I understand it—'

'Enough!' said Friend. 'Obscure civil cases don't interest me, Jerry. But I'm willing to let you tell me, in simple language without a bunch of foaling around—'

Jerry laughed. 'Hey, I like that—'

'It was an accident! I'm willing to let you tell me just what you think this has to do with the murder of Van Ness Masterton, even if it isn't my case. I assume this thing was settled to everybody's satisfaction in the appeals court.'

'I don't know about everybody's satisfaction, but it was settled. The court ruled—'

'Never mind that. You think this court case gave somebody a motive for killing Masterton? This Hopper guy maybe? Or somebody from this bloodstock agency? Were they at the party?'

'I don't know. I doubt it. Actually, the way the case was decided Masterton was still the biggest loser. The court of appeals affirmed the lower court's decision in favor of the bloodstock company, but Masterton wound up settling with Hopper to smooth things over. I don't think the parties to the case had any reason to go after revenge. But I think the case was used by Masterton in his party game to stand for the Triple Crown winner, Affirmed. For that purpose, any court case where the lower court's ruling was affirmed would have done just as well. But I think the report was removed by the murderer, who thought looking into the case might lead the police to the motive for the crime. It could have something to do with the incident of gelding the wrong horse but nothing to do with either Hopper or the bloodstock agency. I'm sure I'm right, because when I first thought about this I didn't even know there *was* a case. And now I've found there is. It would be just too much of a coincidence if there was no connection.'

'Jerry, do me a favor when you call Lexington.'

'What's that?'

'Don't mention my name!'

When Jerry reached Morton in Lexington later that Monday morning, he found the Kentucky cop more polite (not taking a friend's liberties) but no more convinced. Jerry wasn't sure whether the matter would be pursued or not. Still, he'd done his duty and could pursue lunch in the backstretch café.

★   ★   ★

Jerry's reception in the lunchroom was no more or less cordial than usual. Obviously, calling the Kentucky Derby (and calling it right) on national radio had not made him an instant celebrity.

Tim Bastian was sitting at one of the tables

121

in the lunchroom as usual. Jerry thought the old exercise rider must spend more time in there than anywhere else, save possibly his living quarters, wherever they were. Certainly he saw more of the faded plastic tablecloths than he did of the Surfside Meadows track.

Jerry joined Tim and offered only trivial racetrack smalltalk until Hortense came over and took their order. Then he gave up resisting his detective impulses.

'I've been thinking about Denny Kilbride...' he began.

'Poor Denny!' Hortense exclaimed. 'Nobody cared about him, and he had to die just when he had a good horse in his barn for a change.'

'Colt didn't do much,' Tim pointed out. 'He's back here again. Not going to try for the Preakness.'

'Do you know anything about Denny's background before he started training out here?'

'He never said much,' said Tim.

'He'd had an unhappy life, that's for sure,' said Hortense.

'Any family?'

Hortense thought about it. 'I think he might have had a son.'

Tim shook his head. 'Denny didn't have no son.'

'I'm pretty sure he mentioned a son.'

'Denny never talked about himself.'

'No, but I got the idea he had a son,' Hortense insisted.

'Denny never had a son,' Tim said, just as definitely.

'Did he ever have any connection with Van Ness Masterton?' Jerry ventured.

'No,' said Tim flatly.

'We'd have known,' Hortense said. 'Somebody would have known. When somebody turns up with that kind of credentials, well. . .'

'Do you ever remember him talking about Van Ness Masterton?' Jerry persisted.

Tim shook his head. Hortense turned and bellowed to the room at large, 'Did Denny Kilbride ever say anything about Van Ness Masterton?'

Everyone was looking at their table now. Jerry was glad there was no particular necessity for secrecy in his investigations. Hortense could be depended on to blow anybody's cover.

'Never said much about anybody,' a younger exercise rider offered. 'But he especially said nothing about Van Ness Masterton.'

'What does that mean?' Jerry said.

'I've known him to turn right around and

leave the room if that name was mentioned.' Several heads bobbed in confirmation.

'I remember him doing that,' Tim agreed. 'But I never thought... Denny was such an old character, you never knew what he might do.'

'What year did Denny turn up out here?' Jerry asked.

Now the whole lunchroom was involved, the interrogation taking on the aspect of a town meeting. Varying estimates were made, but a time about twelve years before was settled on by consensus. The court decision Jerry had found had been handed down ten years ago, but the incident it sprang from had occurred some three years before that, or a year before Denny Kilbride began plying his trade on the West Coast.

'Anybody know what he was doing before he came here?'

No one did. But all agreed he was a fine and experienced horseman. He'd been working with thoroughbreds somewhere, that was for sure.

After lunch Jerry stopped to check with the track's administrative offices to see what they had on Denny Kilbride. The answer proved frustrating.

'You don't have *anything* about Denny Kilbride?' Jerry said unbelievingly.

'Plenty,' said the administrative secretary defensively. 'But not before he came to California.'

'But he was a licensed trainer.'

'He met all the qualifications. But he didn't have to give his whole life history. Of course, if he'd held a training license before, in another state, that would be different, but if he'd been driving a truck or managing a grocery store we wouldn't have to know that here. Would we?'

'No, no. Of course not.' If Kilbride hadn't been working as a trainer, what had he been doing?

In the staff parking lot that afternoon Jerry ran into the same backstretch octogenarian who had first told him about Old Rosebud the horse.

'You're lookin' worried, Jerry.'

Jerry shrugged. 'Why should I be worried, Clyde?'

'I don't know. But I heard you was askin' a million questions about Denny Kilbride today.'

'I wish I knew a million questions about Denny Kilbride I could ask.'

'Well, if it makes you feel any better, there's one thing certain.'

'What's that?'

'Won't be no Preakness murder!'

'There won't?' Jerry said. 'I hope not, but how do you know?'

'Old Rosebud never even ran in the Preakness,' the old-timer said.

All day Jerry would try to figure out the logic of that remark, but it always eluded him.

PREAKNESS 1

'Do you want to take a call from Les Randall?' Susie asked, covering the mouthpiece with her hand and looking at her employer, who was reclining in her overdecorated living room and scowling at the morning paper.

Bettina Winslow looked toward the ceiling in dramatic exasperation. 'That damned fruit.'

'I don't think so,' said Susie judicially. 'I can usually tell. . .'

'Oh, give me the phone,' Bettina said.

Susie handed it over, not concealing her irritation at being snapped at. Mrs Winslow had been in a bad mood, edgy and nervous, ever since the day of the Masterton murder, barring a few hours of Derby-day euphoria. True, she had been beleaguered by the press but, still, having such a big win should have kept her happy for a week or two at least.

'Hello, Les,' Bettina said, turning on the customary media charm like a tap.

'Just a few quick questions this morning, dear.' The Englishman had been checking in every day. 'When will you be arriving in Baltimore? Where will you be staying?'

'Pepperpot is bedded down at Pimlico with his trainer right now, Les. Isn't that the important thing?'

'You underestimate the fascination the beautiful owner of a classics winner has for the public, darling.'

'I'd rather not have my movements publicized, Les.'

'Certainly not. My readers, being safely across the Atlantic, don't care a fig which Baltimore hotel you'll be lying in anyway. But I want to know where I can reach you for confirmation and denial and all that sort of thing.'

'All right. I'll tell you, not for publication. I'll be at the Sorenson.'

'The Sorenson! What a small world! Everybody seems to be staying there. It's Baltimore's Horsy Hilton, for this year anyway. Well located for Pimlico, of course, just off the Northern Parkway, but the downtown area is reputed to be quite beautiful. They've made great strides in urban renewal, I hear.'

127

'Very true, Les, but it's all close.'

'And when will you get in town?'

'I expect to arrive on Thursday. But you needn't meet my plane, darling.'

'Old Rosebud killer have you quaking in your boots?'

'Don't be ridiculous.'

'It looks as if Pepperpot will be a fairly strong favorite. And you know what happened to the Derby favorite's owner...'

'You have such good taste, Les,' she said, restraining her anger.

'I'm a British journalist, my dear. Well, cheerio. See you in Baltimore.'

She slammed down the phone. 'I get so sick of that man, I could puke.'

'But you're so nice to him,' the maid pointed out. 'Even when you say "Don't be ridiculous" your voice drips honeysuckle.'

'Things are bad enough without antagonizing the press.' Bettina picked up the newspaper she'd been looking at before the call came. 'Pepperpot will be 2–1, it says here. Kind of generous. They have the Canadian horse at 5–2, and I can't see him getting within a mile of Pepperpot at the distance, can you?'

'No idea,' said Susie, who didn't pretend to follow racing even casually.

'Tall Sequoia they have at 3–1. He beat us

on the coast. I fear that horse a lot more than any of the others.'

''Cept Old Rosebud?'

'Susie, I don't need that from you!' Bettina tossed down the paper. 'My husband would rather sleep with horses in Baltimore while I lie here...'

'You have your own preferences in that line.'

'Will you remember your place for once?'

Susie was astonished. The outrageous had always worked before, and she was sure it was expected of her. 'My place? My place, did you say?'

'Oh, don't get on some racial high horse. You know what I mean. You work for me. I employ you. I think I'm a good employer. God knows, I never object that you spend every off moment making people nervous with that goddam camera of yours. I welcome your frankness about the clothes I wear, and you cay say what you want about my face and my body, but my personal life is none of your concern!'

'That's something new,' said Susie. She walked out of the room, well shaken but hiding it as best she could. Bettina Winslow had never been anything but glad to have her trainer-husband out of the way for days at a time. But this time, while he was out, no one else was in. And if Bettina had any personal secrets she was concealing from her omniscient maid it was the first time.

★ ★ ★

While his contemporaries were converging on Louisville, Gotham City was back in his stall at Aqueduct. He would sit the present dance out and look ahead to the race all New Yorkers knew in their hearts was the *real* classic, the Belmont Stakes. Metaphorically, that is, he sat and looked ahead. Literally he stood most of the time and looked principally at the four walls of his stall, eating, sleeping, and enjoying the increasingly frequent visits of his owner.

Carol Masterton seemed to be around every day now, having shifted her base of operations from Kentucky to Manhattan. She never interfered in the training of her runners, never questioned Horace Nurock's methods or decisions, but still her visits made the trainer nervous. Truthfully, he was never as comfortable around owners as he was around horses.

This particular morning, the Wednesday of the Preakness week, the wheezing Acton Schoolcraft came plodding along behind her.

She smiled at Nurock, a smile that should

have melted him. She patted Gotham City's nose. The big chestnut seemed to be getting attached to her. Horace was in favor of owners who liked horses, but overly chummy ones made him all the more uneasy.

'How's he doing?' she asked in a no-nonsense tone.

'Just fine. He'll be ready to go.'

'Do we have a prep for him before the Belmont?'

Horace named three stakes on the eastern seaboard that Gotham City had been nominated for, all of them to be run in the three-week period between the Preakness and Belmont.

She merely nodded. 'Use your own judgment. I don't mind. But he probably should have a race of some sort, shouldn't he?'

'Beautiful animal, Horace, beautiful animal,' said Acton Schoolcraft. 'Will you be in Baltimore Saturday?'

'I'll be right here. Nothing to run there.'

'I have nothing to run there, either,' said Carol, 'but I have some nice invitations. Acton and I are driving down tomorrow afternoon. We'll be at the Sorenson if you need to reach us.'

'Winsome Deb's running here on Sunday,' Horace pointed out, referring to the top older mare in the Masterton string.

'I expect to be back in time for that. Will she win?'

'I wouldn't bet on it.'

Schoolcraft gave a wheezing laugh. 'Horace, your disinclination to bet is legendary. That is not responsive to the lady's question.'

Carol saved Horace a further answer. 'If Horace knew who was going to win, he probably wouldn't have that disinclination to bet.' Though she spoke lightly, she didn't really seem much more relaxed or less gloomy than she had been since Van Ness Masterton's death. 'Horace, there haven't been any more of those Old Rosebud letters, have there?'

Nurock shook his head. 'Not a one. I haven't heard of anybody getting one since— since the Derby.'

'I don't know whether that's good or not,' Carol said. 'Horace, have you ever raced a horse that was owned by a syndicate?'

The question itself, as well as the abrupt change of subject, surprised him. 'Not exactly. But I've sure had horses with a lot of owners.' Some winner's circle pictures looked like the Smith family reunion.

'Acton has been urging me to syndicate Gotham City right now, with the understanding he will continue to race through this year and next. He thinks we would still be guaranteed a good price, and that later on it could be higher but it could also go a lot lower. What do you think, Horace?'

A succinct answer formed itself in Horace Nurock's mind. It was a crazy idea to syndicate a horse as he was coming off a losing effort in the Kentucky Derby when a victory in the Belmont would send his stock soaring again. He couldn't possibly be sold at a worse time. If Acton Schoolcraft, who reputedly never took a false step where money was concerned, was urging such a deal on the owner, he could only be giving her bad advice for his own further enrichment by the potential shareholders.

But 'It's up to you, Mrs Masterton,' was all the trainer said.

'Certainly it's up to me,' she said impatiently. 'I want your opinion, though.'

Schoolcraft said, 'I have pointed out to Mrs Masterton that the colt's value is still very high despite losing the Derby, where everyone knows he was the unfortunate victim of deplorable racing luck. There are many investors who know another victory or two could increase Gotham City's value markedly, so they are willing to pay a price now that, frankly, great as I believe this colt is and can be, represents more than his present worth from any realistic standpoint. By syndicating now, Mrs Masterton is sure to benefit herself while passing most of the risk along to the investors.'

Schoolcraft was attempting to answer Nurock's arguments, the obvious ones, even though the trainer hadn't expressed them. But he was unconvincing.

'It's the whole question of responsibility to the investors that puts me off,' Carol said. 'Remember Devil's Bag? Retired prematurely merely to protect the investment of the syndicate's shareholders, when if he had raced on he might have turned out to be a great horse, the kind of champion racing needs. I may be determined to race Gotham City now, but later on I might be subject to pressure from the shareholders, and from my own sense of responsibility to them, to retire him too early. I really think I'd rather take all the risk myself. I'm not exactly destitute, you know, Acton.'

Schoolcraft wagged his head good-naturedly. 'Of course, you must do as you please. But I promise you I won't give up.'

'I'm sure you won't,' said Carol with a weak smile.

Nurock was glad to hear Carol holding her ground, but she still seemed naïve in her apparent assumption of Schoolcraft's goodwill. Why did she trust him so much? Didn't she realize he was trying to use her? Or maybe she did realize. At least she wasn't going for the syndication deal. Yet. Van Ness Masterton had trusted Schoolcraft, too, up to a point anyway.

'What did you say, Horace?' Carol responded to the trainer's nearly audible mutter.

'I said I think the Peter Pan might be the best Belmont prep for Gotham City.'

'Excellent,' said Acton Schoolcraft. 'A race with a great and honorable history!'

Gotham City playfully nudged his owner's shoulder with his aristocratic nose.

★   ★   ★

Early on Thursday morning, Bill and Arleen Holman parked their rented Pontiac in the horsemen's parking lot just off Winner Avenue and entered the barn area behind the Pimlico grandstand, their credentials carefully checked by a security guard.

'The back side is on the front side?' Arleen asked.

'Part of it's on the back side, but they stable all the Preakness entries in Barn E. That's where Tall Sequoia is.'

'They stable them all together? That seems

funny.'

'Don't forget nearly all the Preakness horses ship in. Hardly any would have been stabled at Pimlico already.'

'Where are the black-eyed Susans?'

'They don't grow this time of year, honey. The ones they use for the winner's blanket are daisies painted in the center with black shoe polish.'

Arleen smiled. 'That could only happen in California.'

'But this is . . . Hey, you knew that all the time.' Bill gestured toward a crowd of people with cameras, TV units and microphones prominent. 'I'll bet that'll be Barn E.'

Barn E was a media carnival, but Pepperpot, as the Derby winner and thus potential (if rather unlikely) Triple Crown winner, was getting most of the attention. The Holmans were able to have a word (most optimistic) with their trainer about Tall Sequoia's chances and to have a look at some of the spotted roan colt's opposition as well. The Preakness, which traditionally drew a somewhat smaller group than the Kentucky Derby with its inevitable moonshooters, would have a field of a dozen, seven of whom had contested the Churchill Downs race. Of the remaining five, the one really unknown quantity, or mystery horse for overwrought journalists, was Beltway Bob, a locally owned and trained colt who had won his only three races by daylight, though against markedly less classy competition.

Bill and Arleen spent a few minutes looking around on the fringes of the media crowd, virtually unnoticed. After their recent experiences, this relative anonymity was simultaneously a relief and an affront. But Abner Kelley spotted them and walked over.

'Welcome to Pimlico,' he said with hand outstretched. 'It looks like a quiet year here. No missing-Derby-winner controversy. No Lasix controversy.'

'No murders yet,' Arleen murmured.

Abner had no answer for that, but he didn't let it dampen his ebullient mood. 'Your charger looks fit and ready anyway. It should be a tough race, very competitive. Of course, the local management is a little unhappy that Gotham City isn't here. And they'd like to have Martin Fine to help the press fill their columns, with or without his horse.'

'Jerry in town yet?' Bill asked.

'I'm picking him up at the airport later this morning. Where are you guys staying?'

'The Sorenson.'

'Well, so's our whole team. What a coincidence!'

'Not really. You recommended it.'

137

'Oh, yeah, I did. A lot of the other owners are there, too. Logical enough, I guess. It's new and beautiful and handier to Pimlico than just about any other hostelry. We'll have to get together for a drink.'

Ab's smiling face turned somewhat somber at something he saw over Arleen's shoulder. She turned around to see that Grant Engle had joined the throng of reporters and photographers.

'How can he be smashed so early in the day?' Abner wondered.

'He's drunk? How can you tell?'

'I can tell. You get to know somebody as well as I'm required to know that turkey and you can spot the little clues. At least he's standing up.'

Bill asked, 'What's his problem? Is he that upset about blowing the Derby finish?'

'Maybe that's it. Hard to say. But if he doesn't snap out of it he won't be able to tell one nag from another by Saturday. They'll all have little spots like Tall Sequoia.'

'Then, we're guaranteed a winner,' said Arleen. 'At least on TV.'

'Isn't it time to give Jerry a shot?' Bill said.

'It may be time at that, but unfortunately there's nothing in Engle's contract that says he has to call every photo finish on the nose or that he can't get pickled between assignments.

Even in his network blazer. Well, if you kids will excuse me, I better go tend my tiny flock.' Abner scurried away with an economical wave.

The Holmans weren't alone for long. A local TV crew had divined their presence and were moving purposefully in their direction.

'Ah, fame,' Bill said with comic resignation. Arleen suspected he really enjoyed it, though it was starting to pall on her. Bill thought the same thing, with roles reversed.

★   ★   ★

The desk manager at the Hotel Sorenson recognized Bettina Winslow as soon as she appeared from behind the lobby's multicolored fountain that Thursday afternoon. She was a startlingly beautiful woman but, more than that, she had an air of importance, as if every step through every opening constituted an entrance. The doorman had completed his welcome to the hotel and received a tip that, judging from his expression, must have been a generous one. A bellman had already taken charge of her bags, and the desk manager had only to supply a key to the suite Mrs Winslow's husband theoretically already occupied, though the trainer had been little seen at the hotel since checking in several days before.

Mrs Winslow was traveling with a quietly dressed, neatly attractive black woman whose firm, determined features gave her a formidable appearance. She was carrying a camera. A secretary perhaps? Surely not a personal maid. Very few people, even the very wealthy, traveled with servants these days.

'Welcome to the Hotel Sorenson, Mrs Winslow,' the desk manager said. He thrust forward the key and a piece of mail that had been waiting in the pigeonhole for room 1035.

Bettina Winslow smiled and took the key and the letter. A faint look of alarm flickered across her face. Strange. The same kind of thing had occurred when he'd handed a similar-looking piece of mail to Mr and Mrs Holman late that morning.

He watched the two women stride away with the bellman. The possible significance of the letters struck him for the first time. He read the papers and watched TV (news and sports only) and was well aware of the Old Rosebud business.

Moments later, there was a telephone call from room 1035. Mrs Winslow sounded upset, on the verge of hysteria even, but maintaining calmness as best she could. He reassured her.

'A gift of the management, Mrs Winslow.

We apologize for any distress we may have caused you. Certainly, we'll have them out of there at once.'

He laid down the phone with a sigh. They should have known. The traditional vase of roses for the hotel's VIP guests had been a bad idea this Preakness week.

★　　　★　　　★

Jerry Brogan had received no letters in the lobby, and there was no vase of roses in his surprisingly small, though efficiently planned and tastefully decorated, room. Minor and temporary network employees did not get the VIP treatment. But almost as soon as he had taken off his shoes and tested the queen-size bed the phone rang. He had a call from California, the desk informed him. Could Donna be calling him in the midst of a busy schoolday?

No.

'Jerry, this is Martin Fine. How's Baltimore?'

'Well, the Baltimore–Washington International is a nice airport, but it's just about like any other airport. The freeways are like other freeways, but they call them beltways. The hotel is nice but hardly distinguishable from any other nice hotel in any other city in the world. The skyline of Baltimore is pretty from a distance, but I can't claim I have the flavor of the place just yet. I just got here, Martin.'

'What about Pimlico?'

'Haven't even been out there.'

'Well, look, Jerry, I'd appreciate any impressions you have of the competition back there. Just keep me posted. Be my spy, huh? I'd like to get back there, but we're shooting Ames on a tight schedule all week and I just can't make it.'

'Late in the year to be shooting a TV series, isn't it?'

'Schedules mean nothing any more, Jerry. These are for fall. Some of these scripts they give me I gotta rewrite from the ground up. It's sometimes tough to be concerned, Jerry. People say I should take the money and run but, as far as millions of people know, Dr Paul Ames is me. What good he can do I do, and if he's garbage I'm garbage. You know what I mean? Anyway, I want to run Doc Paul in the Belmont if he has a chance.'

'He'll have a good chance, Martin.'

'Well, I want you to scout the opposition for me. My trainer is too busy putting bandages on his broken-down platers to tell me anything. And, Jerry, I want to know what they're saying about me back there.'

'What they're saying about you? What do you mean?'

'Some people think I pulled Doc Paul out of the Preakness because I was afraid, spooked by the murder of Masterton. Jerry, you know and I know that's not true. I just do what's best for my horse. But that's what people think, and I don't like it a bit. So I'm trying to make it plain I'll go to the Belmont if Doc Paul runs OK in his race out here. We're either going in the Will Rogers on the grass or in a big overnight race on the dirt, if they can put one together for us. I'd rather go on the dirt right now if we can, and at a little longer distance, but it's a question of digging up a field of horses to run against us. Anybody that knows me knows I'm not scared, and I'd appreciate it if you'd let the people back there know that.'

Sensing a minuscule pause in the actor's monologue, Jerry started to say something diplomatic, but his tongue didn't move fast enough.

'I don't suppose you ever read the *National Onlooker*, Jerry, except the headlines in the supermarket checkstand line like everybody else. Well, their front-page story this week has a picture of me—I don't know how they got it—where I look like I just got frightened out of my damn wits. I don't remember the

143

circumstances of the picture, but it's me all right. And their feature story drips with innuendo that TV's crusading Dr Paul Ames is a cringing coward in real life. I already talked to my lawyers, and they tell me not a thing in the article is actionable, no matter how much it damages my reputation in the eyes of the public. But, Jerry, the crazy thing is, even if I was the chicken they think I am, there's really nothing to be scared of. I'm willing to bet whoever blew Van Ness Masterton away had it in for Masterton, not for anybody else. Whether it was the writer of the Old Rosebud letters that did it or not. I think the letters were a smokescreen, don't you, Jerry? Somebody had it in for Masterton and that's it. Right? Don't you agree?'

'I think you're probably right, Martin.'

'Sure I am. Enough of this crap. So who's going to win the Preakness?'

'Well. . .'

'Pepperpot, Penticton, Tall Sequoia. They don't really impress me, Jerry. Doc Paul would have left 'em back in the ruck if he'd had a little racing luck in the Derby. So would Gotham City, of course, but we'll see about him in the Belmont. I really think we'll be there for the Belmont, Jerry. We'll be a long shot—New Yorkers never take California form seriously—but we'll be there. What about this horse Beltway Bob? What's he look like?'

'I haven't seen him, Martin.'

'Well, have a look. Of course, I can have a look at him myself on TV on Saturday, but I'd like an informed opinion from somebody else first. When you can beat everybody you know about, you worry about the ones you don't know about, don't you? It's human nature. Jerry, I wish we'd gone to the Preakness with Doc Paul. He's on top of the world, and I wish we'd gone there. I sincerely do. I wonder if it's too late. Is it?'

'You mean . . . ?'

'Too late to run him in the Preakness. If we could get a plane out tomorrow. . .'

'Martin, they've already taken entries.'

'Yeah, I suppose so. It's Thursday, isn't it? Anyhow, Jerry, we'll show 'em what we're made of in the Belmont. Look, Jerry, I got to get back on the set. This show we're doing is fabulous. One of our best. Really gets to the heart of the issue. It's about—No, I'm not supposed to talk about it. But it's the greatest social issue of the day, Jerry, and we take a cold, uncompromising look at it. For network TV, Jerry, this will be the most daring, talked-about show in twenty years. Cable wouldn't touch it, it's so hot. But, look, Jerry, if you come across any information I can use, call me collect, or I'll call you.'

Jerry hung up a moment later, as wrung out as he always was after talking to Martin Fine. He knew he'd be hearing from him again, and he hoped he could come up with answers that would help widen the distance between the TV actor and what seemed an inevitable heart attack. How could a person live at such a high pitch?

Jerry looked at his watch. It was another two hours until he was to meet Ab Kelley for dinner. He almost closed his eyes.

The phone rang again. This time it had to be Donna, knowing how lonely he'd be, taking a moment away from play rehearsal to tell him she loved him. He picked up the phone hopefully.

'Jerry? Bill. We're in 723. Come on down to our room and have a drink. We're having a few friends in.'

'Start without me, Bill. I've got jet lag.'

'Between LA and Baltimore you've got jet lag? Come on!'

'I'll try to come by a little later. Many thanks.' Jerry hung up. He imagined Arleen's reaction to Bill's decision to have a few friends in. It was probably half the hotel, guests and staff both. He was glad 723 was several floors away.

After an hour's nap, though, he could stop

146

by and wish his old friends luck.

The phone rang again. Startled awake, Jerry glanced at his watch. He'd actually dropped off for a half-hour, though it had seemed like thirty seconds.

'Hello?'

'Jerry, this is Bettina Winslow. I'm in 1035, and I need to talk to you about something.'

'Oh. All right.' This invitation he wouldn't refuse. 'Right now?'

'Please. If you can come.'

'Sure, I'll be right there.'

Since 1035 was a mere two floors below Jerry's room, his immediate impulse was to go down the stairs, but a search through the maze of corridors on the twelfth floor failed to turn up any that weren't designated for emergencies only. Eventually he found himself waiting rather ridiculously for the elevator to take him the short way down.

Ten minutes after talking to Bettina on the phone, he was knocking on the door of 1035. A fortyish and very attractive black woman answered the door.

'Mr Brogan?' she said, poker-faced but not unpleasant.

'Right,' he said. 'Is Mrs Winslow ...?'

'Come in.'

It appeared to be the royal suite, complete with bar, white deep-pile carpet, plushly expensive furniture, and original art on the walls. The woman opened a door into the bedroom and said simply, 'He's here.'

'Send him in here, Susie,' said Bettina Winslow's voice.

'Sure, why not?' said Susie, giving Jerry a meaningful look.

Jerry didn't know what he was getting himself into, but he welcomed another chance to talk to Bettina Winslow. He walked through the door, and Susie closed it behind him.

'Hi, Jerry. Thanks for coming.' Bettina Winslow was seated in a chair by the bed. She smiled with an effort and directed Jerry to sit opposite her. 'We can ruffle the covers a little later, so we won't disappoint Susie, but I didn't call you in here to make love to me.'

'I didn't think you had.'

'Or you wouldn't have come, right?'

'I won't try to answer that one.'

She looked at him appraisingly. 'Maybe we won't disappoint Susie after all,' she said, with a flicker of her usual manner. 'But I called because I'm worried, and I heard you were in the hotel. I think you're someone I can trust. To give me some advice.'

'Sure,' said Jerry.

She handed across a piece of paper. Computer paper with a message in all capitals from a dot-matrix printer.

THE PREAKNESS COULD BE THE MIDDLE JEWEL ON YOUR TOMB— OLD ROSEBUD

Jerry shrugged. 'Tell the police. Right now. Why call me?'

'You think I should? Have there been others?'

'Probably. I don't know. But the Baltimore police need to know about this. They're providing extra security anyway, but... Tell me something, Bettina, do you know who Old Rosebud is?'

'I haven't the vaguest idea, Jerry.' He believed her.

'Well, do you have any idea why he's carrying on his campaign? Or why he killed Van Ness Masterton, if he did?'

'Certainly not,' she said, less convincingly.

'Weren't you married to Masterton at the time of the Bluesking incident?'

'The what?' Jerry had the feeling it was a direct hit. She couldn't quite conceal it.

'You know what I mean. You must.'

'Bluesking. Some kind of business jargon, isn't it?'

'Sure, I suppose so. But it meant more than that to Van Ness Masterton.'

'Calling you was just like calling the cops,' she shot at him. 'I don't think I want you here.'

'I'm not as comforting as you hoped? What did you want me to do?'

'Protect me. I thought you were the only person I could trust. But I think I'll just lock my door instead. Get out of here.'

'Are you going to let the police know about that Old Rosebud letter?'

'Yes, of course. I'll have to now that I've told you about it. Don't worry. I'll get right on the phone. Now, please leave.'

Jerry left, puzzled. She hadn't been amenable to any probing. Why had she called him? He was big and she was desperate, and she seemed to turn to men other than her husband for comfort, as she'd turned to Grant Engle at the Masterton party. Maybe they would have wound up together in her king-size bed, as the woman called Susie had obviously expected.

Feeling he should have been sorry to miss such an experience (but somehow wasn't), Jerry waited at the elevator for transport to the Holmans' room. He might as well pay his duty call now.

The door to 723 was wide open. It was a good-sized room, if not as large as either of the ones Bettina Winslow occupied, and there were plenty of people with drinks in their hands taking advantage of the Holman hospitality. The crush was such that almost twenty minutes (and a full circuit of the room) passed before he even had a word with one of his hosts.

Arleen greeted him warmly, but her lined forehead looked more worried than ever.

'Is Bill overdoing the hospitality again?' Jerry asked in a stage whisper.

'It isn't that, Jerry. I don't mind that. But look. . .'

She produced an Old Rosebud message identical to the one received by Bettina Winslow.

'Have you reported it?' Jerry asked.

'Oh, sure,' said Arleen.

A bass voice that sounded as if it belonged on the opera stage, or at least on the radio, resonated over Jerry's shoulder. 'Mrs Holman?'

'Yes?'

'How do you do? I'm Detective Alex Sutherland, Baltimore police.'

Jerry turned around to see a tall and powerfully built black man with a thin mustache and a receding hairline. Jerry handed the cop the Old Rosebud message and introduced himself. 'There's something else you should know. Mrs Winslow, who owns the favorite for the Preakness, got the same message. I just came from her suite.'

The detective nodded. 'Wonderful,' he said. 'We have to talk to everybody here, Mrs Holman. . .'

'Everybody? But. . .'

'Everybody you know. And I assume you know these people, don't you? Now, what room is Mrs Winslow in, Mr Brogan?'

'She's in 1035.'

'This is my associate, Detective Krasna. Why don't you show him the shortest way to 1035, Mr Brogan.' The policeman had a cool manner, but there was an undertone of urgency to his instructions. They knew all about the Old Rosebud business in Lexington and were on edge.

The door to 1035 was slightly ajar. Krasna knocked on the door and called out, but there was no reply. They entered the room. There was no sign of Susie or her employer. The detective, following a nod from Jerry in the direction of the bedroom door, walked in.

Jerry heard him say, 'Shit!' He sounded more irritated than horror-stricken. Through the bedroom door, Jerry glimpsed the body of Bettina Winslow lying on the floor. He didn't see any evidence of how she'd gotten that way, but he did see the single rose lying by her body.

Donna Melendez, weary from a day of educating young thespians along with less invigorating pedagogical pursuits, kicked off her shoes, swung her feet onto the footstool, and aimed her remote-control tuner at the television set. It was time to see some people with real problems.

The six o'clock news had already begun, and the first face she saw was more than familiar. Jerry? She hit the volume button too hard and filled the room with his roaring voice.

'I can't say anything about that,' he said. He looked harried. 'You'll have to ask the police about that.'

'Mr Brogan, isn't it true you were the first to find Van Ness Masterton's body in Lexington?'

'I was there, but. . .'

'Did you notice any similarity between the two killings?'

'I told you I'm not at liberty to talk about that. It's up to the police.'

The local news anchor man's face came on the screen. 'Repeating, Jerry Brogan, track announcer at Surfside Meadows, is *not* believed to be a suspect in the second of what

153

is becoming a series of murders at the sites of horse racing's Triple Crown races. First victim was Van Ness Masterton, owner of the Kentucky Derby favorite, Gotham City. Today's victim, found strangled in her Baltimore hotel room by Brogan and a Baltimore police detective, is Bettina Winslow, owner of Pepperpot, favorite for this Saturday's Preakness Stakes. Again, the owner of the favorite in a Triple Crown event has become a murder victim. Unconfirmed reports suggest that more anonymous letters from the mysterious Old Rosebud preceded today's tragedy.' The handsome talking head looked down, shuffled a few papers in front of him, and continued dramatically, 'Just in from our network affiliate in Baltimore is a report that Mrs Winslow's maid and companion, identified as Susan Bailey, first reported as missing, has been found and is being questioned by the local authorities for any information she might have about this latest death.'

Donna sat stunned in her chair, wondering if she should ever let Jerry leave town by himself again. He needed somebody to keep him out of trouble.

'Where did the rose come from?' Jerry said suddenly.

It was after midnight. Sutherland, the Baltimore cop, was weary from hours of questioning people in a temporary office discreetly provided by the Sorenson's management. The room was about the size of a walk-in closet in the Winslow suite. He looked across the tiny coffee-table at Jerry with an expression that combined fatigue with suspicion. 'What rose, Mr Brogan?'

'The rose by her body. I saw it through the doorway.'

'You attach some significance to that, do you?'

'Of course, I do. There was a rose on Van Ness Masterton's body, too. You knew that, didn't you?'

'I did, yes. The question is how did you know that?'

Jerry almost stopped himself from pointing out he'd been the one to find Masterton's body. It seemed an odd coincidence that he should be at the scene of both murders, though, of course, he wasn't the only one. And obviously there was no concealing any of this.

'Have you talked to Morton, the Lexington detective who handled the Masterton case?'

'Should I?'

'Of course. Isn't the MO the same here as in Lexington?'

'I don't think so. Masterton was stabbed. Mrs Winslow was strangled.'

'But the flower. . .'

'The flower isn't MO, Mr Brogan,' the detective laughed unexpectedly. 'The folks out at Pimlico are going to be disappointed it wasn't a black-eyed Susan. Sure, sure, I've talked to Morton. We're co-operating. And he told me about you. A race-caller who thinks he's Mike Hammer.'

Jerry had to protest. 'I've never thought I was Mike Hammer. Lord Peter Wimsey, maybe. . .'

'Your physique is all wrong.'

'Tell me about it. But, look, my question is serious. Where did the rose come from? How did the killer get it? Couldn't that help to trace him? Or her?'

'Nice thought, Mr Brogan, but the management provides a vase of fresh roses for all its VIP guests, and the Preakness owners are definitely in that category. This hotel is up to its ass in roses. . .'

'You read F. Scott Fitzgerald?' Jerry asked

offhandedly.

To his surprise, the cop looked astonished, and Jerry knew briefly how Sherlock Holmes must have felt. 'How'd you know that?'

'Elementary. You just quoted one of his best lines.'

'Did I?'

'Paraphrased anyway. In the story, it was daisies.'

'I'll be damned. I didn't know racing people read books.'

'I didn't know homicide cops did.'

'Who do you like in the Preakness, Mr Brogan?'

'Is that an official question?'

The detective grinned. 'No, just a two-dollar bettor's question. I've been wanting to ask somebody all night, but it didn't seem quite appropriate. I'll be out there on Saturday if I can steal the time.' Then his face lit up. 'Hey, maybe I can go out there on duty for once.'

Jerry had never met a cop who followed the races and had hastily generalized that police work and horse-playing didn't go together. He decided to press his advantage. 'I'll give you the winner, if you'll fill me in on your investigation.'

Sutherland snorted. 'Bullshit! You just want to play amateur detective.'

'I've had considerable success in that line, you know,' Jerry said, with marginal accuracy.

'Who's your winner?'

'I'll tell you after you tell me what you found out tonight. I've been stuck in my room watching an old movie waiting for you guys to call me in for grilling.'

'And the old movie probably had some private eye or amateur the dumb cops let in on everything, huh?'

'Unfortunately, no. They don't show movies that old very much any more. Was Emmett Winslow in the hotel at the time his wife died?'

'As far as we know, he was still out at the track. That's what he said. We're checking, but I'd say he had a pretty good alibi.'

'Did he seem broken up at his wife's death?'

'I'd have said indignant more than anything. Some people are hard to read, though. My partner thought he was a cold fish, but I had the idea he took it pretty hard in his way.'

'What about the people at the Holmans' party?'

'Practically nobody we can eliminate there, including the Holmans themselves. Everybody was in and out and nobody keeping much track.'

'The murder had to be committed between the time I left Bettina and the time I went back to the apartment with Detective Krasna. That wasn't even half an hour. It seems incredible you couldn't eliminate anybody in such a short timeframe.'

'It does, huh? Well, maybe you can help us out. Who in the room could you account for for the whole time you were there? Who was in your sight all the time?'

Jerry reviewed the chaotic scene in his mind. 'Nobody, I guess.'

'The Holmans are friends of yours, aren't they?'

'How'd you know that?'

'It's the flatfoot's business to know these things, Mr Brogan. So who's going to win the Preakness?'

'I'll be glad to tell you in a minute. Did Morton fill you in on my theory about the court case?'

'He did and he didn't. His account was a little sketchy. Like an atheist explaining the Holy Trinity.'

'Then, let me give you the true believer's version,' Jerry said, and he outlined his ideas as logically as he possibly could. They still came out sounding far-fetched even to him.

'Yeah, that's just great,' said Sutherland.

'It couldn't be the key to the whole thing?'

'I don't say it couldn't be. But I'd give you good odds it isn't. It's too far out. There are plenty of ways to approach a case like this, and we'd exhaust eleventeen of 'em before we got around to investigating some old case report that might not even have been there. I guess that's why we cops need gifted amateurs to help us out.'

'Police detectives everywhere keep telling me that same thing in different ways,' Jerry said.

'You haven't given me your Preakness winner yet, Mr Brogan.'

'That's coming, but there might be another way I can help you.'

'I'm still looking for the first way.'

'Have you looked into the crossover beween people staying in this hotel and ones who were there when Van Ness Masterton was killed in Lexington? That should give you a manageable group of suspects.'

'If you assume the same person took out Masterton and Mrs Winslow. But, yeah, we've explored that up to a point. You were there.'

'Yes.'

'And the Holmans.'

'Right.'

'And Abner Kelley, the TV guy. Another friend of yours, right?'

'Have you been talking about me all evening?'

'Oh, you loomed large, Mr Brogan. Very large.'

'I usually do.' Jerry was beginning to realize there were entirely too many old friends in the closed circle of suspects he was trying to provide. 'What about reporters? Have you come across a character called Les Randall?'

'Englishman? Pain in the ass?'

'I see you have. Is he registered at the hotel?'

'No, but he's been around a lot. Including this afternoon. Did you have anyone else in mind?'

'Masterton's widow must be in town. Is she by any chance. . . ?'

'In the building. We've talked to her. Also a heavy-breathing old geezer named Acton Schoolcraft. Doubt if he'd have the energy to strangle anybody, but sometimes they fool you.'

'What about the Masterton trainer, Horace Nurock?'

'Still back in New York, they told me.'

'I think that may be all,' Jerry said. Then another element occurred to him. 'What did Bettina Winslow's maid have to tell you?'

'Was she at the Masterton party?'

'Not that I know of, but was she able to give

you any leads on what happened to Mrs Winslow? She was there when I left, and the killing couldn't have taken place very long after that.'

The detective grinned. 'You're going to give me the Preakness winner, right, Mr Brogan?'

'Absolutely. Assuredly. Guaranteed.'

'OK, then, I'll tell you what we got out of the maid.'

The detective paused dramatically and leaned forward with a confidential air.

'Not a damned thing, that's what we got out of the maid. Said she was given the night off quite abruptly and unexpectedly after you left. She took it. Didn't know anything about her employer's death until she returned to the hotel.'

'Can she prove it?'

'Not really. Very vague. Said she went to a movie. She had a ticket stub, but you know how much that proves. She could describe the movie she went to see, too, but it's been out a long time and she easily could have seen it back home, so that didn't prove anything, either. She was alone, and of course nobody saw her.'

'She's a good-looking woman.'

'Mr Brogan, Baltimore is full of good-looking women of all colors. And I'll be able to impress one of them just as soon as you give me the Preakness winner.'

Jerry, who hadn't been thinking about the horse race at all for several hours, searched his mental files. 'Tall Sequoia,' he said, trying to sound as confident and authoritative as he could. 'Can't lose.'

'Tall Sequoia?' Sutherland seemed disappointed. 'The California horse?'

'He's ready to roll.'

'He's your pal's horse. I don't think you're objective.'

'You asked for the winner. I gave you the winner. If you don't like the one I chose, I can't help it.'

'I heard from a guy whose brother's a hotwalker out at Pimlico that Beltway Bob is going to come in at a price.'

'The Maryland horse. And you call me provincial? It comes down to this: do you believe me or some hotwalker's brother?'

'Well, I have to believe you. Look at the energy I expended just to get this information.'

'I thought I was helping you with your investigation.'

'Sure. You've been a big help, Mr Brogan. You'll be in town how long?'

'Through Saturday. I don't expect any longer than that.'

'Fine. No problem. Just let us know where you can be reached.' The detective stood up and extended his hand. 'I'll probably see you on Saturday, Mr Brogan. If any more questions come up you might be able to help me with, we can talk about it then. And I do hope you gave me the right horse.'

Jerry thought Sutherland put a slight note of menace into his last remark. But the cop had a sense of humor. He was just kidding. Of course he was.

Back in his own room, Jerry stretched out on the bed, expecting at last to get a little sleep. But his bedside phone shrilled once more.

'Hello.'

'Jerry. Ab Kelley. I need you.'

'You don't need me, Ab. There are no races to call in the middle of the night.'

'I don't need the race-caller. I may need the wrestler. This is no joke. It could be serious. Meet me in the lobby right away. Please.'

'OK.'

★   ★   ★

It proved to be a rescue mission. Ab had received a call that somebody in a network blazer was causing a disturbance in a bar a few blocks from the hotel. Jerry and Ab didn't

164

need three guesses as to who it was.

In the back seat of the cab, Jerry asked, 'Was Engle in the hotel when Bettina was killed?'

'I don't know. I assume so.'

That was one more person who had been both at the Sorenson tonight and at the Masterton party. Jerry wondered if Sutherland had talked to him.

Ab and Jerry got out of the cab in front of the Sir Barton Pub, a rather high-toned tavern decorated in British style. Ab told the driver to wait. Inside, everything seemed quiet enough, a few patrons nursing drinks at the bar or in dark booths along the opposite wall. Though they weren't wearing network blazers, the bartender seemed to know who Ab and Jerry were immediately. He nodded them toward a doorway at the back of the room that said 'Employees Only'.

A small balding man ushered them into a cluttered office. 'My name's Carpenter. I'm the owner and manager. I got him out of sight as soon as I could. I didn't want any embarrassment for you people. After all, you're our guests.'

Grant Engle sat in a chair opposite the paper-strewn desk, his chin on his chest, snoring loudly and fragrantly. In his vomit-soiled network blazer he would have made a fine publicity shot to go to all the affiliated stations.

'My brother-in-law used to work for your network. You might know him. Vince Capucci?'

'Uh, no,' said Ab, looking balefully at his first-string race-caller. 'What did he do?'

'He was a weatherman at your station in Keokuk, Iowa. You never ran into him?'

'Never did. Tell me, Mr Carpenter—'

'The wife and I love your Tuesday-night line-up. I'm never home, but the wife tapes it on the VTR and we watch it Sunday afternoon.'

'Mr Carpenter, we really do appreciate your efforts here. What exactly did Engle do? You said he was creating a disturbance.'

'Well, he was and he wasn't. It wasn't really his fault, Mr Kelley. I don't really blame him. He was drinking pretty hard. He had too much, that's for sure. And he seemed depressed.'

'What about?' Jerry asked.

'I think he called the wrong winner in the Kentucky Derby, didn't he?'

'But that was two weeks ago. He couldn't still be sulking about that, could he?'

'I don't know.'

'What time did he get here?'

'About nine o'clock.' Well after Bettina

166

Winslow had been murdered, Jerry mused. Could that have set Engle off on his latest drunk?

'Did he say anything about—?'

Ab Kelley interrupted. 'Mr Carpenter, what exactly happened?'

'It was nothing really. He just made some cracks about Baltimore that some of my less refined customers took exception to. There was a tiny little scuffle. Nothing really. Once I smoothed things over and hustled Mr Engle back here and explained things to my other patrons, there was no problem. I knew that most of your network contingent was at the Sorenson, Mr Kelley, and of course I knew your name from the broadcasting trades, so naturally I called you.'

'Were the police called in?'

'Oh, no. Not necessary. Not at all.'

'Was there damage?'

'Minimal really. A hundred dollars' worth, perhaps. My insurance covers it.'

Ab Kelley quietly drew five hundred-dollar bills out of his wallet and passed them to the tavern-owner. 'Mr Carpenter, we very much appreciate your handling this as discreetly as you did.'

'Quite unnecessary,' said Carpenter, pocketing the money none the less. 'Mr Kelley, Vince Capucci and I have an idea for a new approach to local television weather. Vince was trying something of the kind in Keokuk, but there was a misunderstanding with the station manager that really was none of Vince's doing. . .'

'I'm afraid that's not in my department, Mr Carpenter.'

The tavern-owner whipped a card under Ab's nose.

VINCENT CAPUCCI/ALVIN CARPENTER
Operatic Weather Consultants

'Perhaps if you could show this around in the right office, it might help. Vince has a beautiful voice, but Keokuk just wasn't ready for it.'

Ab said all the right things, committing himself to nothing, and soon he and Jerry were carrying the unconscious Engle out a back door and through an alley to the waiting cab.

On the way back to the hotel, a panting Ab said, 'Jerry, thanks for coming along. I didn't need you to put down any violent people, but you did help me carry Engle. I sometimes think we've been carrying him for years. But please don't start playing detective on a network PR mission. We got this nicely swept under the rug.'

'Ab, Grant Engle's a suspect, like anybody else who was both at Masterton's and here tonight. Did the police talk to him before he went on his bender?'

'I don't know. Maybe not. Do you think he already knows about Bettina Winslow?'

'Probably. They knew each other rather well, to put it mildly, and her death might have been enough to set him off.'

Ab leaned back in the seat. 'Scandal. Juicy, dirty scandal. We'll probably replace Martin Fine on the front of the next *National Onlooker*. I can see I'm going to have to nursemaid this crumb from now to post-time on Saturday. Shouldn't have let him out of my sight tonight. This afternoon he'd slept a few hours and was just about over his previous toot, but I guess he got his second wind.'

'Look on the bright side, Ab. You may have stumbled onto the next New Wave in TV weather reporting.'

Ab gave a perfunctory chuckle. 'You expect that kind of thing in Hollywood, but this is Baltimore. With my luck, the hotel doorman will have a script he wants me to read.'

In front of the Sorenson, Ab left the cab to negotiate a way to get Grant Engle back to his room without going through the lobby.

★　　★　　★

Jerry spent most of Friday at Pimlico, gathering information and getting ready for his call of Saturday's big race. In the morning, a Preakness tradition went on as usual, though undoubtedly somewhat more subdued than in most years: the Alibi Breakfast, where owners, trainers and jockeys of Preakness entries met the media in one big press conference. Observers with a morbid turn of humor enjoyed the irony of the event's title.

Les Randall was a prominent questioner at the Alibi Breakfast, his upper-crust English drawl constantly trying to inject references to police matters that the Pimlico publicity people would have preferred to keep off limits.

Grant Engle was present, with Ab Kelley in close but nervous attendance. Though he seemed enveloped in gloom, Engle was sober and caused no problems.

Emmett Winslow did not appear, and no one denied the trainer had a good excuse. An assistant predicted victory for Pepperpot, who would indeed run despite the tragic death of his owner. The trainers of Beltway Bob and Penticton asserted their chances just as definitely. The trainer of Tall Sequoia hedged, but his confident manner belied his cautious words.

Jerry's breakfast tablemate was Miles Waters, a likable fellow who was a correspondent for the London *Times*. Jerry noticed Waters winced every time his journalistic colleague Les Randall opened his mouth.

'Quite a British presence this year,' Jerry remarked.

'I'm here on holiday actually, but my editor will expect some travel pieces from me,' Waters answered. 'That fellow is a bit of an embarrassment, I must say.' Jerry had no need to ask who he meant.

'You know him?'

'All of Fleet Street knows him.'

They compared notes on the problems of and differences between English and American racing in much more amiable tones than Jerry's similar exchanges with Les Randall. As the breakfast drew to a close, Waters took his leave with a cryptic remark. 'Don't worry, old man. We'll forgive you.'

What did he mean by that? Jerry wondered. That Britain would forgive America for draining off so much good English bloodstock probably.

Though Jerry had enjoyed the breakfast, he enjoyed a visit to Barn E more. Looking over Tall Sequoia, he reflected that he might just possibly have made a friend for life on the

Baltimore police force.

Back at the hotel, he received a welcome telephone call for once.

'Brogan,' Donna said, 'I saw you on the news, and you looked like a mad-dog killer run to earth. You're getting yourself in trouble again.'

'I'm not in any trouble. The cops let me go. I didn't even have to post bail.'

'When's the next one, Jerry?'

'The next what? The next murder?'

'The next out-of-town horse race.'

'Three weeks from tomorrow.'

'And that's in New York, right?'

'Yep. Belmont Park.'

'Well, I'm about to convince the principal of Richard Henry Dana High that, in the interest of better-informed pedagogy, his drama coach ought to take in some of the Broadway theater season, and all it will cost him is a couple of days off.'

'Donna, that's the nicest idea I ever heard.'

'Can we go jogging in Central Park?'

'If we must. I think we can get up more speed after sundown.'

Only a few euphoric moments separated Donna's call from Martin Fine's.

'Who's doing this, Jerry? Who's killing people? They're trying to ruin racing. I didn't get into this to get scared out of it, Jerry. I don't scare easy, but this is getting to be too much for me, I don't mind telling you.'

Jerry had been getting ready for Fine's call, pithy comments on all the Preakness entrants fully formed in his mind. So it figured. When Jerry wanted to talk about the murder, the principal cop wanted to talk racing. When Jerry wanted to talk racing, the owner of Doc Paul insisted on talking murder.

'I'm just thankful for one thing,' the TV actor went on. 'The killer seems to be going after the owners of favorites, and I don't have to worry about being favored in New York, do I? With a California horse?'

'I don't think so,' Jerry said. 'How's the show going?'

'I'm at home,' the actor said disgustedly. 'We had to shut down yesterday. Some damn starlet gets the flu, and we have nothing but her scenes to shoot. Bad planning in my opinion but, then, I'm only the star. I have to come to the Belmont now, Jerry, whether Doc Paul is on top of his game or not. My whole reputation is riding on this after that tabloid article. They ought to do something about that sheet, Jerry. I'm for the first amendment, and censorship to me is the dirtiest four-or-however-many-letter word in the English language. We did a great show on that, raked in the Emmys. But somebody said on the set

173

the other day, "Jefferson never read the *National Onlooker*." Funny, huh? Did you see the article, Jerry?'

'No.'

'Here's something else. Whose byline do you think is on the article? None other than our friend Les Randall. I didn't even notice it the first time I read the thing, but after they peeled me off the ceiling I had a closer look. When he was just publishing his crap in England, he was a pain in the ass, but now he's broadened his readership and he's a pain everywhere. Have you seen him back there?'

'Yes, he's making his presence felt.'

'Can't you do something to get him away from the races, Jerry? Anything. Give him a hot tip that John McEnroe is hiding out in a condo in Newport News. I'll tell you, if I see that guy again, he's going to be more than sorry. I'm an easygoing guy, but I take only so much.' Fine paused for a breath. 'So what did the Preakness horses look like?'

'I forget.'

PREAKNESS 3

Pimlico on Preakness Stakes day offered the same kind of festival atmosphere as Churchill

Downs on Kentucky Derby day. Tents, flags, bare chests and bare legs seemed to fill the infield. The grandstand, glassed in against winter weather that seemed a world away today, was equally packed. Early crowd estimates were something over 80,000. The field had taken to the track to the strains of 'Maryland, My Maryland', which Jerry thought sounded suspiciously like 'O Tannenbaum'. Overlooking the track from the radio booth, Jerry sketched the scene for his listeners and did his best to submerge thoughts of murder.

'They call it the Middle Jewel of racing's Triple Crown, and for many years it offered a larger purse than either the Kentucky Derby or the Belmont. The Preakness, run at a shorter distance of a mile and three-sixteenths, doesn't have the universal glamor of the Derby or the testing aura of the Belmont, but it has one advantage: just about every year, it has one entry that can be advanced as a potential Triple Crown winner. The existence of this selling point explains why the Pimlico folks get so upset on those rare occasions that the owner of the Derby winner chooses not to come to the Preakness. Most recent to do that was Gato Del Sol in nineteen eighty-two, but back in the fifties no less than three Derby winners, all California-based, skipped the Preakness: Determine, Swaps and Tomy Lee.

'Today the potential Triple Crown champion everyone will be watching is Pepperpot, who ran in the colors of the late Bettina Winslow and is now owned by his trainer, Emmett Winslow. Pepperpot was regarded as something of a trial horse for the major three year olds throughout the winter and early spring, but in Louisville he stepped to the front of the class, and today he'll try to enhance his place in racing history.

'Intersectional interest remains strong, possibly stronger than in any Preakness in history. From the midwest, Pepperpot; from the Southwest, Valid Point; from the northeast, Rocking Wagon; from the immediate Baltimore area, Beltway Bob; from the southwest, the very quick sprinter Mop Away; and from the far west California's Tall Sequoia, Washington's Brave Invader and western Canada's Penticton.'

Jerry rattled on, pouring out stats and anecdotes to bring his listeners up to post-time. Out of the corner of his eye, he could see the TV team grinning away on a monitor, notably the alleged expert known as Artie (the Line) Prince. Supposedly a former Las Vegas odds-maker, Artie was advanced by the network as the world's leading authority on all sports, particularly the betting aspects thereof. In an unpolished Bronx-accented delivery, he made *ex cathedra* pronouncements about horse racing that made absolutely no sense to anyone who really knew the sport. Most irritating was the fact that he had somehow picked Pepperpot to win the Derby, presumably with a hatpin.

Being on the scene saved Jerry from listening to whatever drivel Artie was offering the homes of America. Who wanted to be on TV anyway? Radio is the vehicle of the sportscaster's real art, as Ab Kelley kept assuring him. True, most of the listeners would be in cars, but Americans spent a lot of time in their cars.

The tote board was giving some interesting messages. The favored Pepperpot was held at a reasonable 9–5. But Beltway Bob had been made the second choice at 3–1. It might have looked like local chauvinism, but Maryland bettors aren't stupid. Odd, though, that Penticton, second in the Derby blanket finish, was offered at 4–1; with Tall Sequoia, fourth under the same blanket, an even bigger bargain at 5–1. Rapscallion, whose cough had caused him to miss the Derby, was fairly well regarded at 7–1. Rocking Wagon and Valid Point, quite likely the closest sixth- and seventh-place Derby finishers in history, were listed at 12–1 and 10–1 respectively. After that it was boxcar figures on the other five runners, including Derby starters Mop Away (50–1) and Brave Invader (90–1).

Detective Sutherland had dropped by the booth briefly, apparently just to say hello, and had assured Jerry he had bet not quite the mortgage but still a sizable amount on Tall Sequoia and he liked the generous odds just fine. Of course, he didn't imply there would be any reprisals if the spotted roan failed to get there first. So why did Jerry find himself wondering about the accommodations at the Baltimore jail?

As the dozen horses were loading into the Pimlico starting gate, the tote board changed odds one last time. Pepperpot held at 9–5, but Beltway Bob came down to 5–2, Penticton to 7–2, and Tall Sequoia went up a tick to 6–1, while Rapscallion dropped a tick to the same odds. The Holmans' charger wasn't getting much respect. Still, if he won at that price, it could make one Baltimore cop happier still.

The rumbling crowd noise reduced itself to that eerie hush that precedes the opening of the gate in a classic race. All twelve seemed to be standing still, ready to go. The flagman raised his red cloth.

'They're off!' Jerry told his audience of motorists. 'Mop Away goes right to the front.

Beltway Bob, away well, is second. Rapscallion is third, followed by Pepperpot and Tall Sequoia.'

As the field passed the grandstand, the southwestern colt extended his lead to three lengths. The jockeys on the contenders didn't seem to be worried about Mop Away. Beltway Bob and Rapscallion, both front-running types with considerable natural speed, were kept under a stout hold. The Canadian colt Penticton had dropped to the back of the field, while the rest were in a tight bunch.

'Turning into the backstretch, it's Mop Away pulling away by six, seven, now eight lengths. Rapscallion is second a half-length. Beltway Bob is third by a length and a half. Brave Invader is fourth by a head. Pepperpot is fifth on the outside by three-quarters of a length, and Tall Sequoia is sixth along the rail.'

Jerry thought they could be making a mistake letting Mop Away pull away by so much. If any of the Triple Crown tracks favored speed, it was Pimlico. Many had won the Preakness wire to wire, including some lightly regarded outsiders. But the colt was going so fast over a course not noted for speed, the quarter in twenty-two and one, the half in forty-six, it seemed he would have to be a superhorse to stay out there.

'Approaching the far turn, it's still Mop Away holding away by five lengths. Rapscallion is second by a head, Beltway Bob third, and here comes Pepperpot, moving well on the outside, and Tall Sequoia coming through on the rail. They're followed by Brave Invader and Valid Point. Turning for home now, it's Mop Away by three and a half lengths. Tall Sequoia on the inside is now second by a half-length, with Pepperpot looming up third, and Beltway Bob between them holding on in fourth. Mop Away went the six furlongs in one/o-nine and two, only a tick off the track record for that distance!'

What happened was inevitable. Mop Away, having given the fans and his few backers at 50–1 their thrill, stopped cold. Straightening out for home, he still had a length on the field, but he was weaving like a weary prizefighter. He drifted out from the rail, leaving room for both Tall Sequoia and Pepperpot to move inside him. Beltway Bob had dropped farther back in fourth place.

'Down the Pimlico stretch, it's Tall Sequoia and Pepperpot head and head. Now Tall Sequoia pulls away to a half-length advantage. Pepperpot is second, then a gap of three lengths to Beltway Bob, Valid Point and, coming very late, Penticton. It's the spotted roan, Tall Sequoia, now opening daylight on the field. He leads by two, three lengths. Pepperpot is still second. It's Tall Sequoia wins the Preakness by two and a half lengths! Valid Point got up for second by a head, Pepperpot third, and Penticton fourth, followed by Brave Invader, Rocking Wagon and Beltway Bob.'

Mop Away had dropped all the way back to last after his brilliant fractions. Jerry wondered if the jockey had done anything but sit there.

During the commercial, the engineer turned to Jerry and said, 'I guess Engle got that one right.'

Jerry grimaced. The TV people were still the stars. Engle would have had to be really out of it to have missed the winner this time. After the commercial, Jerry wrapped up his broadcast as quickly as the network's time constraints dictated. Then he leaned back and tried to enjoy the success of his friends the Holmans on the TV monitor.

'Old Artie the Line missed that one,' the engineer remarked. 'He picked Pepperpot right out in front of God and everybody.'

'Even an idiot can't be right every time,' Jerry said with satisfaction.

'Nobody had Tall Sequoia, did they?'

'I picked him!' Jerry protested.

'I didn't hear you.'

'Well, no, I didn't do it on the air. I'm an objective reporter, not a tout.'

The monitor showed a track employee who had climbed to the top of the cupola behind the Preakness winner's circle. The weathervane there had the figure of a horse and jockey on it, and longstanding tradition called for the painting of the jockey's silks in the winning owner's colors as soon as the result was declared official.

Arleen Holman, looking beautiful, happy and a bit dazed, was responding to an interviewer's questions.

'How does it feel to have the favorite for the Belmont?'

A grim look crossed her face briefly as she realized the implications of the question. 'That's up to the bettors, not me,' was all she replied. Bill joined the picture and fielded an equally astute query about his plans for additional security protection.

Jerry was disgusted. Tall Sequoia wouldn't be favored for the Belmont anyway. He didn't have the bloodlines that suggested a mile-and-a-half horse. Gotham City would be favored for the Belmont. Everybody knew that. Even Old Rosebud must know that.

★   ★   ★

In the Pimlico pressbox after the race, Jerry was accosted by Les Randall. 'Your old chums did it, eh? Jolly good race. None of these nags would last the first mile at Epsom or Newmarket, of course.'

'Of course, of course. Well, *Lezzz*, I understand you're branching out in your journalistic efforts.'

'Oh, you must mean my little piece in the *National Onlooker*. Yes, my masters do allow me a spot of freelancing from time to time. Your Yank tabloids have next to no interest in the gee-gees, but they're quite enthralled with Martin Fine, though I'm deuced if I know why. I was just in the right place at the right time to sell them the right story. Did you enjoy it?'

'Nobody reads *National Onlooker* articles, Les. Their headline-writer, of course, has one of the largest reading audiences in the history of journalism, but the articles themselves? Only in a very slow-moving checkstand line.'

'People keep telling me things like that, Jerry, but honestly, if none of those hausfraus in the market queue ever bought a copy, the rag couldn't stay in business—now, could it?'

'I don't know. It might be worth it to the food chains to subsidize the *Onlooker* just to have something to entertain the customers in line. You doing any more pieces for them, Les?'

'Oh, I don't think I really ought to say, do you? But the Old Rosebud business is simply fraught with possibilities.'

'Just how did you get the way you are, Randall?' Jerry said, working hard on his sneer and wondering how offensive he could get without getting a rise out of the thick-skinned Englishman.

'Heredity, I suppose. I come of a splendid family, Jerry.' Randall seemed to pause to consider his next remark. 'My mother's people made quite a nice fortune manufacturing chimes from elephant tusks—exploiting countless poverty-stricken natives along the way, I have no doubt. Actually, though, I am a bit of a family skeleton. You see, my father was my uncle. It could give a chap a Hamlet complex, but I escaped somehow. What's your lineage, Jerry?'

'I must be descended from one of the elephants. Excuse me, will you, Les?'

Extricating himself from the Englishman, Jerry found Abner Kelley at the other end of the pressbox.

'Did Engle do OK?' he asked.

'Oh, yes, yes. He's already drowning his lack-of-sorrows in the bar, but he got through the race just fine. We might be better off if he gave the network a real excuse to fire him.

Well, now, Jerry, I think this would be a good time to suggest a class reunion to our old schoolmate Bill Holman, don't you? I believe the Preakness management traditionally sends the winning owner a case of champagne.'

On their way out to follow up on that idea, they were stopped by Detective Sutherland, who thanked Jerry for making his day.

'Not in the Dirty Harry sense, I hope,' Jerry said nervously.

The cop laughed. 'If you have any more ideas to share with us, Mr Brogan, just give me a call down at headquarters.'

Jerry knew he didn't really mean it. Impressed as he was with Jerry's handicapping, the cop couldn't really think being able to pick horses qualified a person to pick murderers as well.

BETWEEN RACES 2

The Belmont Stakes is traditionally run three weeks after the Preakness, giving the Triple Crown iron-horse candidates a slightly longer breather before taking on their longest test. Jerry Brogan, from his office at Surfside meadows, made several calls during the first week to the Lexington and Baltimore detectives working on the two Triple Crown murders. The *first* two, as he couldn't help thinking of them. Morton and Sutherland were both tolerant and relatively cordial—Sutherland especially, for reasons not hard to understand—but Jerry gathered they regarded his interest as a minor nuisance rather than a major source of assistance. As far as he (and the watchful, salivating news media) could tell, the police were making no particular progress in finding the Old Rosebud killer. The newspapers, magazines and TV networks deceptively appeared busier, finding a new angle on the case nearly every day. The Blueskying factor, as Jerry came to think of his own theory, still didn't seem to loom large in the investigators' plans.

'Maybe I should go public with it,' he said to Donna one Friday evening, six days after the running of the Preakness. They were sitting in deckchairs outside his Surfside Beach apartment, watching the sunset and the crashing waves.

'With what?'

'That court case. I don't understand why the police haven't seen how important it must be.'

'I can understand it.'

'You can?'

'Sure. You may be right, Jerry. I'm not

186

saying you aren't. But if there was a reprint of that court case in Masterton's house that night nobody ever found it. And, as you've said yourself, the actual parties to the case have no motive for the murders and no apparent connection to the victims. For the police to follow up on your idea, they first have to follow your reasoning that *a* court case must have been there on the table, then make the leap of faith that says that particular court case must have been on the table.'

'It's not a leap of faith,' Jerry protested.

'That's not how you see it, but it is how they see it. It just doesn't sound like the real world of criminal investigation to them. It's too remote, too crazy.'

'So I'm crazy?'

'Not you, Jerry, just your ideas.'

'How comforting. But there are other reasons for thinking the gelding of Blueskying is connected to the murders. What about that Old Rosebud letter where the threat was spelled out with the names of famous geldings? And when I pointed that out to Bettina Winslow she suddenly went from light and airy to damn-near terrified! Donna, there is a connection. That incident ties the whole thing together, and if the police won't look into it I'll do it myself. Or, like I said, I could go public.'

'Go public,' she echoed in a dubious tone.

'Sure, tell my story to the papers or TV. If the killer has reason to think someone is onto the connecting link, it may prevent further murders.'

'Or send Old Rosebud after you.'

'Why should Old Rosebud come after me? All I know will already have been published. He'll have nothing more to fear from me.'

'But will he know that? Or she? I should add. Jerry, don't make yourself a target. I didn't decide to go to New York with you so we could get blown away together, you know. Theorizing is fun, but—'

'Fun, you say? Fun? We're talking about murder here, murders that have been done and murders that can be prevented. This isn't fun.'

'Come on, Jerry. You're approaching this just like a party game.'

'Not me. It's Old Rosebud who's approaching it as a party game, and it's Old Rosebud that's having all the fun. Maybe I'll call Les Randall and tell the story to him. I can't stand the guy, but he can get it to a wide audience now that he's working for the *National Onlooker*.'

'Jerry, please don't!'

He could tell in the fading light that Donna looked genuinely worried. He pinched her bare thigh playfully. 'You're taking this seriously, too, aren't you?'

'I don't want you playing games with a maniac, Jerry. I want you to stay out of it.'

'Even if I can keep somebody from getting killed?'

'More likely you can get yourself killed. And, anyway, isn't it obvious to everybody that it's the owners of the favorites this nut is after?'

'You've been reading the papers. That may just have been a coincidence. It may have nothing to do with his motive.'

'I hear Bill and Arleen have brought Tall Sequoia home and aren't going to run him in the Belmont. Is it because . . . ?'

'Because they're frightened of Old Rosebud? No. If the killer goes after the owners of favorites, they'd have nothing to worry about, because Tall Sequoia wouldn't have been favored for the Belmont anyway. Gotham City will. There are two good reasons for not running Tall Sequoia back there. Number one, there's nothing in his breeding to suggest he wants to go a mile and a half. Number two, he's a bleeder.'

Donna looked shocked. 'A hemophiliac?'

'No, no, it's nothing that bad. But some horses are prone to bleed through the nose under stress. Little blood vessels burst. It's not too serious, but it does affect their performance.'

'I can see it would,' said Donna, whose tenuous approval of horse racing was constantly being assailed by new unpleasant details.

'They're given a blood-pressure drug called Lasix to ease the problem. Out here, Lasix for horses in training is quite legal, and Tall Sequoia gets it regularly. He could also run with it in Kentucky and in Maryland, too, once he was certified as a bleeder by the state veterinarian. But Lasix, along with every other kind of medication for racehorses, is outlawed in New York. Under some circumstances, the Holmans might take a chance and run him without it for one race, but that problem combined with the fact they probably wouldn't have won the Belmont anyway led them to bring him home instead. Old Rosebud had nothing to do with it.'

'If you say so. Jerry, whatever this nut's motives are, I really don't think your asking for more personal publicity is a good idea.'

Jerry sighed. 'I suppose not. It may be a better idea to keep looking for proof of the connection myself. Then I can present it to the police and let them take it from there. Of course, I thought I was already doing that, but I guess I do owe them something a little more substantial.'

'Be careful doing that, too.'

'Miss Kitty, how can I do my job as marshal if I'm busy bein' careful all the time?'

Donna snuggled closer. The sun had disappeared into the Pacific. 'I don't want to lose you, Brogan.'

'I don't want to be lost.' He kissed her. 'Besides, I can do all my digging by a relatively safe, rarely poisoned or booby-trapped appliance called the telephone.' He kissed her again.

Donna wrapped her arms around Jerry's shoulders and pressed herself against his chest. 'The what?'

'The telephone.' A shrill ringing came from the inside of the apartment, as if to illustrate his statement. 'It's also easily ignored,' he said hopefully.

Donna pulled away and smiled. 'One of your friends may be in need of you. You must answer,' she said.

'*Ninotchka*, right? Your Russo–Swedish accent is adorable,' Jerry said. He resignedly lumbered off to answer the dial-toned dictator.

'Hello, enemy of romance,' he said into the mouthpiece.

'Jerry, nobody ever called me an enemy of romance.' Martin Fine, whose voice was getting more familiar than ever these days. 'I love romance. I even read Harlequins, but nobody knows that, so don't nose it around. Maybe we should do a show on that, though, something light, a change of pace, about a guy that reads paperback romances and hides it from his friends. I don't mean Dr Paul Ames will be the guy, though. It'd ruin his image. Ruin mine, too. But, as they say on the radio, that's not what I called about. Look, are you going to be out at Hollywood Park tomorrow?'

'Well, I wasn't. . .'

'Can you and your lady come and be my guests for the day? Doc Paul is running his Belmont prep in the fifth race, and I thought you'd like to see it. I'd like your opinion, too. Of his Belmont prospects, I mean. We're pretty well committed to go, unless he really falls on his face tomorrow, but I'd like to have an idea of his chances. Can you make it? My trainer says it's as tough a field as they could muster against us, but I really don't know. It's a hard thing to gauge.'

'I'd like to come, Martin, and I'll ask Donna if she can join us. How are things going? Any interesting mail?'

'Old Rosebud letters? Nah! Nothing new on that front. I think the guy's scared to mail any more. With all the interest focused on them now, anybody'd have them in the hands of the cops ten minutes after they received one. And the police experts would be sure to nail him one way or another if they have enough clues to go on. We won't see any more Old Rosebud letters, Jerry. 'Course, it's not really the letters we're all worried about, is it? Not that I'm worried about it. Old Rosebud doesn't scare me, whatever the *National Onlooker* and their limey stringer might think.'

'Did Randall actually talk to you before any of his stories?'

'He's tried, Jerry. He tries to get to me umpty-ump times a week, but I won't talk to the bastard—which, as you know, is not like me. I do like to talk. I really do like to talk, and I even like to talk to the media. Where would a public figure be without them anyway? But I'm through talking to Randall. He'll print what he wants anyway. The hell with him. He'll probably try to approach me at the track tomorrow, but I have my ways of discouraging him. So we'll see you, huh?'

'Sure,' Jerry said, wondering who made up the 'we'. He thought he recalled the actor was married, but Mrs Fine (if she existed) certainly stayed out of the limelight.

★　　★　　★

'We' was not a girlfriend or wife but a muscular bodyguard who effectively kept Martin Fine separate from anyone he wanted to avoid—a category which was essentially confined to Les Randall. Fine's clubhouse box was ideally located, and Donna seemed to be enjoying her first visit to Hollywood Park, a beautiful plant that had been renovated not long ago for the inaugural running of the rich Breeders' Cup races. But she and Jerry both were growing slightly weary of Fine's nervous and continuous monologue by the end of the fourth race and were somewhat relieved when the actor and his burly shadow left them to go talk to Doc Paul's trainer and jockey (and possibly to the horse himself) in the saddling paddock.

'That guy wears me out, Jerry,' Donna said, sipping a tall glass of iced tea. 'Such energy, though. He must have been even more of a commanding presence on stage than he is on TV. How can a man his age stay so continuously hyper without keeling over?'

'He can't keel over. He'd be afraid of missing something.'

'Do you ever watch his show?'

Jerry suddenly raised his hand for quiet. The public-address announcer was giving the result of the Peter Pan Stakes in New York, which had been run that same day. 'The winner was Financial Whiz.' A startled gasp came from those in the crowd who recognized the significance of this information. 'Fortuitous finished second and Gotham City was third. The winner paid fourteen dollars, and the running time was one/forty-eight flat.'

'I'll be damned,' said Jerry. 'Gotham City beaten again. I wonder what his excuse was this time. Of course, it was just a prep, but that horse isn't supposed to lose anytime he steps on the track.'

'Well, is the horse that beat him any good?'

'He's attracted quite a bit of attention back there, and he didn't run in the Derby or Preakness, so he's fresh. That's the kind of horse that quite often jumps up and takes the Belmont, by the way. But the horse that ran second, Fortuitous, was beaten way off in the Derby and finished well behind Gotham City. Maybe the colt's not right. It'll make the Belmont all that much more interesting, I guess.'

'Maybe we should change our mind,' said a voice over Jerry's shoulder. He turned around and shook hands with a grinning Bill Holman.

Arleen, who was with him, shook her head with a worried smile. 'No, we won't,' she said.

'Just kidding,' Bill said. 'We may send Tall Sequoia after the Californian. It's been a while since a three year old won that. Hi, Donna.

We don't see you out here very often.'

'Only when I'm asked,' Donna said.

'This is the crusading Dr Paul Ames's box, I see,' said Bill. 'I don't envy you guys watching the next race with him. He sometimes gets a little nervous when his horses run.'

'He gets more nervous than he is ordinarily?'

'Oh sure,' said Bill. 'He might start chewing on his chair. It's a habit he picked up from chewing scenery all these years.'

'You two seem in a cheerful mood today,' Jerry observed.

'The Preakness purse makes us both cheerful, and having Tall Sequoia safely home makes Arleen very cheerful.'

'We won't see you in New York, then,' Jerry said. He almost added that they'd be safely out of the line of fire, but it didn't seem to be a tasteful remark somehow.

'Don't count on it. We're going to fly back to watch the Belmont anyway.'

'Bill doesn't want to miss any parties,' Arleen said, but there was no apparent venom in the observation. 'We'll make all the big events till the money runs out.'

'It won't run out,' Bill said. 'As long as we stick to other people's parties, huh? Seriously, we're on our way now. We're in the big time.

And, anyway, we're not really going just for the parties. Arleen has family back there. She just thinks like a native Californian. You're going back, too, Donna?'

'Sure. I'm *hoping* to get in some theater.'

'The Belmont's always good theater.'

'I don't think my principal will recognize that fact.'

Jerry explained, 'She wants to do professional in-service training and keep an eye on me at the same time.'

At that moment, Martin Fine returned from the walking ring to greet his fellow owners chummily.

'Did you hear that? They beat Gotham City. Is that something or not? My little horse is looking terrific. And look at that tote board. Even money! My little horse should be 1–5 with this bunch.'

'This is a pretty tough field,' Bill observed. Hollywood Park had managed to muster four horses—Questing Willie of the Derby field and three lesser-known but promising three year olds—to go against Doc Paul at a mile and an eighth, once around their recently enlarged oval. The race had a purse of fifty thousand dollars, big for an overnighter, and though it wasn't officially the feature race of the day it was attracting the most interest.

'A pretty tough field by everyday standards,

197

sure,' Fine agreed. 'But there's not a classics horse among them, unless you count Questing Willie, which I don't. Doc Paul will take them apart. You kids stay right here and watch.'

Fine proved to be more accurate than he knew. The late Denny Kilbride's sprinter went to the front as expected, with Doc Paul running freely and easily in third place. By the midpoint of the backstretch, Doc Paul had already passed Questing Willie and breezed effortlessly into the lead.

While Martin Fine was watching his charger, Jerry Brogan watched Fine. The actor really did seem to be getting more excited than was good for him as he watched the race. While any neutral observer could see that Doc Paul was having things all his own way, a dozen different emotions seemed to cross his worried owner's face during the running. By the stretch, he was registering the same reaction as the rest of the crowd; utter amazement.

Doc Paul, his jockey sitting on his back without the slightest thought of going to the whip, was two lengths ahead as the field straightened out into the long Hollypark stretch. As the yards went by, he steadily increased his advantage. Five lengths, six lengths, ten, twelve, fifteen. Doc Paul crossed the finish line, eased up, with his nearest opponent, a genuinely talented and promising runner named Royal Cavalry who had been second in support from the bettors, twenty lengths behind. The time on the board was only two-fifths of a second from a track record set when the Hollywood Park course had been much faster than it was today.

The crowd roared approval as the watchers in Martin Fine's box merely gaped.

Bill Holman said, 'Martin, I do believe that was the most devastating performance I ever saw. Your horse looked like Secretariat out there.'

The others expressed congratulations to Fine, who still looked stunned.

'Shouldn't you be going down to the winner's circle?' Donna prompted.

Suddenly Fine seemed to realize what had happened. Letting out a whoop, he started a leaping run down the aisle, nearly forgetting to let his formidable bodyguard run interference.

*   *   *

His owner didn't ask Gotham City how he was feeling the morning after the Peter Pan Stakes. This was understandable since she knew he couldn't give her an answer. Instead, she fed him his usual carrot, cast worried, puzzled looks in his direction, and sought reassurance from his trainer.

'He's OK, Horace?' said Carol Masterton.

'Just fine. He cooled out great, and he's sound as a dollar.'

'Did he eat?'

'Like a horse.' Neither of them smiled at, or even seemed to notice, the trainer's mild joke. 'He acted just like always.'

'You're not worried about him?'

Horace Nurock shrugged. 'You're always concerned when a horse doesn't beat a field he should. But I think he just had an off day, came up a little short.'

'We go ahead after the Belmont?'

'It's up to you, but I say Sure. He needed a race, and now he's had one. He'll be ready.'

She nodded. 'I hope so. I love this horse, Horace. I want him to be everything he can be.' After a pause, she said, 'Acton Schoolcraft is still trying to convince me to syndicate Gotham City.'

Though old Schoolcraft hadn't joined them this morning, Horace had felt his presence hovering around the barn, waving money and a syndication contract. After yesterday's debacle, immediate syndication was an even worse idea than it had been after the Derby. Horace wanted to urge her not to do business with the crafty old devil, though it was really

200

none of his business. But Carol Masterton was standing there looking at him, and he had to say something. 'You never wanted that,' he found himself blurting out. 'Why are you even considering it now, Mrs Masterton?'

She smiled sadly. 'It sounds ridiculous, Horace, coming from someone who will have lunch at the Algonquin this noon, but in a sense I need the money. The fact is that my husband's various business ventures weren't going nearly as well as I'd thought. After his death, all kinds of cracks have shown up in his so-called empire. Not the thoroughbred end, but some of the other things he'd invested in. I'm afraid he planned the syndication as much for financial reasons as for any of the reasons he gave. I may have to do the same thing, but I'll avoid it if I can.'

Gotham City watched his owner walk away. He really did feel pretty good. Given the power of speech, he could not have explained his performance of the day before, any more than Van Ness Masterton could have explained his bad investments or most humans can comprehend the wellsprings of an off day.

*   *   *

A few barns away, Emmett Winslow was

scowling at the telephone in his makeshift office. He rarely stabled horses in New York, and he didn't like the whole East Coast atmosphere. He'd brought Pepperpot and a few others up from Baltimore because it seemed the next logical step, but he felt the pull of his usual bases of operations in Kentucky and Illinois.

'I can't say yet,' he told the telephone.

'I understand Pepperpot came out of the Preakness in good condition,' said the English-accented voice on the other end of the line.

'He did. He's fine. But that don't mean I'll run him in the Belmont. I'll make a decision in a few days.'

'Mr Winslow, is your late wife's maid, Susan Bailey, still in your employ?'

'I thought you called to talk about horses, Randall.'

'Yes, and I believe we have been, but I'm trying to reach Susan Bailey, and—'

'I said I'd talk to you on the condition we'd talk about horses.'

'Surely, but all I want to know is where I can reach Susan Bailey. Is she still in your employ?'

'Susie is not still in my employ. I don't seem to have much use for a lady's maid. But the police in Baltimore know where she is, and if you want to talk to her I think you better ask them.'

'Certainly. That's very helpful. Thank you very much. Mr Winslow, I know you've been silent about your wife's death. I was wondering if—'

'I've been silent about my wife's death because I don't know anything about my wife's death and I don't have anything to say about my wife's death. Except she was my wife, and she's dead, and I'd much appreciate being allowed to mourn in my own way. You ask the police any questions you have about police things. Now, was there anything else you want to know about Pepperpot or any other four-legged animals?'

'Mr Winslow, have you received any further—?'

'No, I damned well have not received any more Old Rosebud letters, and I'm sick of hearing about that.'

'I was going to ask if you had received any further invitations to run Pepperpot on the West Coast.'

'I'm sure you were. Good morning, Mr Randall.'

★   ★   ★

In the second week between the Preakness

and the Belmont, Jerry tried to make good his promise to find more of a connection between the case of *Cranstone Bloodstock Company vs. Hopper* and the Old Rosebud murders. He did it mostly by telephone, also as promised. He used his racing connections to talk to some of the people who had worked at the Masterton farm at the time of the Blueskying incident. One possibly significant fact he learned was the odd disappearance of the farm manager who'd taken most of the blame for the mistake: Percy Mayo. What had become of Mayo? No one seemed to know. After the Blueskying incident, he'd disappeared faster than a losing mutuel ticket. Jerry sensed that if he could find Percy Mayo he might learn something that would lead him to Old Rosebud.

What kind of a guy was he? Quiet. Kept to himself. What did he look like? Ordinary. Did anybody have a picture of Mayo? Well, he'd been camera shy. Was there anybody around the Masterton farm who liked to take pictures, who might have gotten a candid shot of Mayo? Well, his best informant said, there was that 'colored woman' who worked as Mrs Masterton's maid. She was a real shutterbug. Susie was her name. Susan Bailey? Don't know her last name.

Jerry's next call was to Sutherland in

Baltimore.

'I need to get a hold of Susan Bailey,' Jerry said.

'That sister is in heavy demand, Mr Brogan.'

'She is? By who?'

'Press and TV mostly. Your friend Les Randall would love to talk to her. We know where she is, of course, but we're doing our best to respect her privacy.'

'Look, you know I'm not trying to give her unwelcome publicity. But I'd like to talk to her.'

'And why is that? Are you still trying to solve these murders on your own?'

Jerry bit back a sarcastic response. 'I'm not trying to cast any aspersions on the abilities of professional police, but I think the fact that so many different police forces are working on this—'

'All two of us?'

'It should be four. Lexington, Baltimore, New York and Surfside.'

'Well, that last pair isn't doing us much good. Anyway, what's your point?'

'I know you're all quite capable, but I think you're losing the big picture by having to concentrate on your own turf.'

'Our own turf. No pun intended?'

'Look, I'm following up on things nobody

else seems willing to follow up on, and as soon as I know anything at all useful I'll tell you, I'll tell Lexington and, whether they want to hear me or not, I'll tell New York and Surfside. I'll save you guys even talking to each other. Now, can I talk to Susan Bailey?'

'What is it you want to find out?'

'Who was responsible for the mistaken gelding of Blueskying.'

'I think we know that. I can even remember his name. The farm manager. Guy named Percy Mayo. Morton of Lexington told me.'

'I didn't know you'd even gone that far. You must have been more impressed with my theory than you let on.'

'Not at all, but we do try to be thorough, Mr Brogan, and I have a superfine memory for names.'

'And have you found Percy Mayo?'

'I haven't been looking for him.'

'Has Morton? Has anybody?'

'I don't think so.'

'Has it occurred to anybody he might have some connection with the case?'

'It seems pretty tenuous to me, Mr Brogan. Of course, the Kentucky cops checked out the scene at Masterton's stock farm at that time, but you only dig so far on a wild goose chase.'

Jerry thought the mixed metaphor was intentional but wouldn't give Sutherland the satisfaction of stopping to admire it.

'How about it? Do I get to talk to Susie?'

'I'll tell you what I'll do. I'll call her, tell her you want to talk to her, and if she wants to talk she can call you. How's that?'

'I guess it'll have to do.'

'But I want something in return.'

'What's that?'

'Why, the Belmont winner. What else?'

'I thought you Maryland partisans lost all interest when the Preakness is over.'

'Not this year. I may be going up there as a consultant to the New York police or something—and, anyway, there are ways of getting a bet down. So who's it going to be?'

Jerry thought fast. 'This may not sound scientific, but in the Belmont you always look for a horse with a one-word name that begins with a C.'

'You're kidding.'

'No, really. Just look at history.' Jerry fumbled for a Belmont Stakes press guide under a stack of correspondence on his desk and started flipping the pages. 'Crusader in nineteen twenty-six...'

'Nineteen twenty-six!' Sutherland moaned.

'Hear me out. Then there was Citation in 'forty-eight, Capot in 'forty-nine, Chateaugay in 'sixty-three, Caveat in 'eighty-three. It works even better if the horse didn't even start in the Kentucky Derby or Preakness. There was Cavan in 'fifty-eight. Then there was Coastal in 'seventy-nine. In nineteen eighty-two there was Conquistador Cielo. I know that's two words, but it counts because they both start with a C. Of course, all good systems are selective, and you don't have a horse that qualifies every year, but this year you do. The winner will be a horse called Collate. Very fresh, very promising. He can't lose.'

'OK,' said Sutherland dubiously. 'Can't argue with an expert, I guess.'

'Of course not. Now, get on the phone to Susan Bailey as fast as you can, please. Have her call me collect.'

Sutherland chuckled. 'That may not be necessary.'

An hour later, Susan Bailey did call, and Jerry learned the reason for Sutherland's amusement. She was staying with her sister in Santa Ana, no more than an hour's drive from Jerry's Surfside Meadows office. When Jerry explained what he was looking for, a face-to-face meeting seemed in order.

On the way out to the parking lot, Jerry reminded himself to check out his improvised system for picking Belmont winners in a little more detail to see if it really worked. As it was, the 'eighty-three winner's name was the operative word: caveat.

★   ★   ★

Susan Bailey's relatives had a large house and a family to match in a long-established and well-integrated part of the city. A ten-year-old girl, to whom Aunt Susie seemed still to be an exotic curiosity, showed Jerry into the front room.

'I hope I can help you, Mr Brogan,' Susie said in a no-nonsense tone.

'You seem a little friendlier than the first time we met.'

'That was when I thought you were Mrs Winslow's latest john.'

'It was lucky I left that hotel suite before you did, or the police might have taken me for Mrs Winslow's latest killer.'

She shivered. 'I thought they were measuring me for that part. But you want to see my pictures, don't you? I always liked photography. Mrs Winslow used to hate my carrying my camera around and snapping pictures in all my spare moments. I think she was afraid I was after some kind of information to blackmail her with.'

Was she being funny? She spoke unsmilingly. This poker-faced woman was very hard to read.

'Did you mention this interest to the police?'

'I would have if they'd asked me. They sure asked me plenty about the murder of Mrs Winslow. The story I told 'em was perfectly true. But it just happened to be one I'd seen used over and over again in old mystery movies and TV, and so had they. The TV and newspaper people were after me, and once the police were through asking me the same questions forty-seven times and had said they were through with me I decided to come out here to rest up and try to figure out what to do next. My sister and her husband are nice people, but it's difficult for me to be around them. He's an architect. She teaches college. They're no smarter than me, but I'm just that old stereotyped black maid. I think I embarrass them.'

Jerry essayed a comforting smile. 'You hardly strike me as a stereotyped black maid.'

She returned the smile fleetingly. 'I damn sure tried not to be. I always told Mrs Winslow what I thought. That was what she wanted. And I kept taking my pictures, even if that was what she didn't want. I didn't like her really, but she was an interesting woman. And she sure led an interesting and busy life.'

'Let's see the pictures.'

'Sure.' The pictures were not in an album

but in a big envelope, presumably the same one she'd got them back in after developing.

Jerry looked at them all carefully, scanning them for familiar faces.

'That's Grant Engle,' he said, pointing at one of several people on horseback in one of the shots.

'Oh, yeah, he was around a lot in those days. Came to stay for weeks at a time.'

'Was he involved in some kind of business with the Mastertons?'

'I think he was, yeah.'

'Was he around at the time they gelded the wrong horse?'

'I don't remember. I never knew much about that. I was a house slave,' she added with more bitterness than humor.

There were plenty of shots of the Mastertons. The pictures were good, but few were very informative. Then a face he knew very well leaped out of the photograph, a stableworker holding the bridle of one of the Masterton thoroughbreds.

'Who's that?'

Susie looked at the picture. 'The guy you're looking for, Percy Mayo. I could never get him to pose for me, but I got him a couple of times when he didn't know I was around. At least I guess he's recognizable there, huh?'

'He's recognizable all right.'

211

'You know him?'

'By another name.'

'Do you know where he is? Can he help you?'

'No, I'm afraid it's a little late for that.'

It was the man Jerry and the southern California racing colony had known as Denny Kilbride.

BELMONT 1

On the Wednesday afternoon before the running of the Belmont Stakes, Jerry sat beside Donna on a half-empty DC-10 heading for New York's Kennedy Airport. She had never been there before and was filled wth excited anticipation. He had been there a few nerve-shattering times and was still stewing over the frustrations of the amateur sleuth. It made him a less than ideal companion.

'Why don't you watch the movie, Brogan?'

'I ate your lunch. You can watch my movie.'

'I can't eat airplane food. It all tastes of plastic to me.'

'I couldn't watch this movie anywhere. Movies went down the tubes when you couldn't tell them from TV commercials any more.'

Donna sighed. 'Jerry, I want to enjoy this weekend.'

'I thought you came to nursemaid me.'

'Is that why you're acting as childish as possible? If your cop friends don't appreciate your Ellery Queen shtick, don't take it out on me.'

'Yeah, you're right. I'm sorry. But I thought I'd cracked the case, Donna. First I called Wilmer Friend with the Kilbride connection. "You did a nice job, Jerry," he said, "and it may help in the investigations back east." And I asked him, "What about your murder?" and he said Denny Kilbride was a suicide and there was no reason to think anything else. Then I got on the phone to Morton in Lexington and Sutherland in Baltimore, and they patted me on the head and thanked me for my help.'

'What did you want them to do? Were you expecting a medal?'

'No, but they always act like they know everything already.'

'Maybe they do.'

'They don't know who sent the Old Rosebud letters or who killed Masterton and Bettina Winslow.'

'Neither do you. Do you?'

'Not yet. When I told them that Grant

Engle had been closely associated with the Mastertons around the time of the Blueskying incident, they told me, oh, sure, of course, they already knew that. They didn't seem to attach any importance to it.'

'Do you?'

'It could be important. Who knows? He was near at hand for both of their murders.'

'The question is how near. I'm sure the police are doing their job, Jerry.' She looked at her watch, which she had switched to New York time at the earliest opportunity. 'We ought to be there in plenty of time for tonight's curtain.'

'I hope so,' Jerry said dubiously. Donna had arranged tickets for them for three different Broadway plays on the next three nights. Jerry had thought trying to see something their first night was cutting things rather fine, but Donna had a naïve faith in the timeliness of transportation schedules.

One of the flight attendants crept down the semi-darkened aisle, lowering her head to keep from blocking the movie screen, and crouched by Jerry's seat.

'I'm sorry if we're getting too loud. . .'

'No, no, not at all, Mr Brogan. There's a passenger up in first class who'd like to have a word with you, if you wouldn't mind.'

'Who?'

'I'd rather not say. He doesn't want anyone to know he's on board if he can help it.'

Jerry gave Donna's knee a conciliatory pat and followed the flight attendant.

Donna leaned back in her seat, debating whether to put the uncomfortable earphones back on. Jerry was right about this movie. But, damn it, she was determined to enjoy New York.

★　　★　　★

'Jerry, good to see you. I thought I saw you at the airport, but I didn't get a chance to say hello, and a guy in my position can't be too conspicuous. Especially not at the moment.'

Martin Fine darted his eyes around the nearly empty first-class section of the plane. His watchful bodyguard was seated a few rows away, to the rear. Fine looked even more worried than usual, and he didn't wait for Jerry to ask why. 'Jerry, I looked forward to coming to the Belmont to take it easy, have a good time and watch my little horse run his best. But have you been reading the paper this week? Everybody's falling over themselves making Doc Paul the favorite.'

'You should be flattered, Martin.'

'Flattered? Oh, yeah, sure, flattered. Van Ness Masterton owns the favorite for the

Derby. He gets killed. Bettina Winslow owns the favorite for the Preakness. She gets killed. And now my colt, Doc Paul, is the favorite for the Belmont, and it's clear as can be I'm the next victim. But I should be flattered. Right.'

'You had to expect it, Martin. That race at Hollywood the other day was awesome.'

'Jerry, you and I both know he beat nothing. He beat nothing with great style and in great time, but nothing is still what he beat. He's got no business in the world being the favorite for the Belmont, Jerry. He's a nice colt and I love him, but the favorite for the Belmont? It's like the guys that make the betting lines have it in for me, you see what I mean? They have the power to choose a victim, and nobody should have that power.'

'Maybe the New York Racing Commission will decide to call off all betting on the Belmont, so the killer can't claim another victim,' Jerry said.

'That's really funny, Jerry, and when all this is over remind me to laugh, will ya? When I decided to take the colt back there, I was all ready for the role of underdog. I love the role of underdog, Jerry. I've built a career on it. But I've been doublecrossed. I mean, who ever heard of these snobby New Yorkers making a horse the favorite for the Belmont off a California race? Oh, I know his Derby race was impressive. It impressed the heck out of me, too. But he didn't win the Derby, and we beat nothing in California. And Gotham City, who everybody thought was a reincarnated Man o' War not too long ago, had almost as much excuse as we did in the Derby and is coming up to the Belmont strong.'

'Right. Off a devastating third-place finish in the Peter Pan.'

But Fine wasn't listening. 'It's just not fair, Jerry. My agent says I should scratch the horse and keep my ass back on the coast, but I'll be damned if I'll do that, Jerry. I'm scared but I'm not that scared, and I want to give this little horse a chance to prove himself. I'll be protected by the police in New York, and the network has hired extra bodyguards for me. I'm a valuable man to them. But, Jerry, who can escape this killer? He seems to get to whoever he wants to get to.'

'You could leave Doc Paul to run but go back to LA yourself, Martin.'

'And look like a coward to the whole world? I try not to be on the front page of the *National Onlooker* more than once a year if I can help it. Besides, this nutty killer can get you wherever you are. If I can buy a plane ticket, so can he. And if that little horse wins the Belmont in my colors I want to be there to see it. They can't rob me of that pleasure, Jerry, killers or odds-makers or anybody.' Fine drew a breath. 'I was glad when I found out first class was practically empty on this flight, Jerry, but now I'm getting lonesome. This guy,' he said, nodding his head toward the bodyguard, 'is good at his job but not a stimulating companion. Let me buy you a drink.'

'No, I better get back to Donna. . .'

'Donna's on the flight? Bring her up here and we'll have a drink.'

'Well, Martin, neither of us bought a first-class ticket. I don't know if. . .'

'Look, Jerry, that doesn't matter.'

As it turned out, it didn't. The small screen's intrepid Dr Paul Ames had the flight crew eating out of his hand, and one of them cheerfully went back to summon Donna. Jerry spent the next few hours half-listening to a spirited two-way discussion of Broadway, off-Broadway and off-off-Broadway theater. Before Jerry was able to find out if there was yet a level called off-off-off-Broadway, it was nearly time for the plane to land at Kennedy.

*　　　*　　　*

Jerry and Donna were back in their seats some fifteen minutes before the scheduled time of arrival. Martin Fine, who was to be spirited away in utmost secrecy from plane to hotel, had expressed the hope he'd see them at the races. Donna glanced at her watch and expressed guarded optimism.

Then came the announcement that a slight problem earlier in the day had led to congestion of incoming flights at Kennedy, and the plane would have to spend a little while in a holding pattern over the airport, awaiting its turn to land. 'We have our place in line, and it's only a matter of time,' said the pilot cheerily, 'so please settle back and relax.'

Donna was philosophical. 'We should still make the curtain. Of course, we may not have time to get any dinner first, but I'm not really hungry, are you?'

Jerry shrugged. 'I was hoping for something.'

'Brogan, you had two lunches on the plane.'

Finding that hard to counter, Jerry shifted attention from his stomach to hers. 'But you didn't have anything. You really should eat, Donna.'

'I'll eat, I'll eat. After the show.'

The landing delay stretched out to an hour, but the DC-10 finally touched down. Jerry observed that it was raining in New York. It seemed appropriate to his mood.

On the longish walk to the luggage-claim

area, Donna asked, 'How long does it take to get from Kennedy to our hotel?'

'Maybe forty-five minutes. It'll depend on the traffic.'

She made a face. 'Figure another hour to get checked in and changed and walk to the theater. . . . We may miss a little of the first act. But I know the story. I'll fill you in.'

By the time they had their luggage, Donna had revised her estimate to the whole first act.

As they came out of the terminal, Donna spotted an empty cab approaching the traffic island across the way. 'See if he's free, Jerry. I'll stay here with the bags.'

Jerry splashed across the road, risking death (he felt) with every step.

'Sure, jump in!' the driver said, swinging open the door. Jerry darted back to Donna, and the two of them rushed across with their bags.

Some kind of uniformed functionary had approached the cab and began shouting at Jerry, 'You can be arrested for this. You can be jailed and fined for doing this.'

'What's he talking about?' Jerry asked the driver.

'Don't pay no attention to him. Just jump in.'

'You'll be sorry,' said the functionary. 'You'll be fully prosecuted for this. This is going to cost you people.'

A split second after Jerry and Donna were both in the back seat of the cab, and an instant before the door was closed, the cab made a screechingly defiant U-turn and was on its way to Manhattan. Looking back, Jerry and Donna finally noticed a long rank of waiting cabs on the other side of the island and realized their driver had jumped the line.

'That guy was threatening us,' Jerry said indignantly.

'He can't do nothin' to you.'

'Can he do anything to you?' Donna asked.

'Don't worry about it.'

'Why was he threatening us and not you?'

'He knew I wouldn't pay no attention to him, but he thought you folks might. Welcome to New York.'

Jerry was fairly wrung out by this time, but nothing seemed to dampen Donna's sense of wonder at the Big Apple. As the cab made its way across the Triboro Bridge, Jerry said, 'Remember that movie *The Out-of-Towners*?'

'Sure,' said Donna. 'And the city of New York performed *magnificently* in that movie. Everything that happened to Jack Lemmon was his own fault.'

Jerry didn't remember it that way. He'd have to catch the movie again the next time it turned up on TV.

Early in their stay, Jerry decided it was enough just to survive the few days in New York. No amateur detective work. Just this city was enough of a wall to bang his head against, without banging it against the wall of police indifference as well. After the first day, he found to his surprise he was enjoying himself immensely. Or, more to the point, he was enjoying Donna enjoying New York. The city held a certain fascination for people in theater, the arts, publishing, journalism, and certain other fields that no amount of noise, rudeness and inconvenience could quell. Though broadcasting was at least marginally one of those fields he was fairly immune to the mystique himself, but at least he could appreciate its hold on others.

Donna, with her impeccable taste in drama, had chosen their tickets well. Even the Wednesday-night Act 1 was worth straining for. Their absurdly expensive but network-subsidized hotel room was nice (far from the dilapidated fleatraps of Jerry's earlier visits), and even making love in New York seemed to hold a special cachet, albeit with the usual Californian lover.

Mornings, Jerry did his duty at Belmont

Park, gathering material for his Saturday broadcast. Though he acquired a good seat for Donna for Saturday and the Belmont Stakes itself, she stayed away from the Long Island plant the two preceding days. Afternoons, she demonstrated what she had learned about the subway system, and they hit as many standard New York tourist attractions as they could fit in. By Friday, they at least thought they knew the ins and outs of Manhattan like natives. To Jerry's relief, they never found time to try jogging in Central Park.

Jerry's cinematic referent had shifted at least temporarily from *The Out-of-Towners* to *On the Town*.

★   ★   ★

Friday night, Jerry lay on top of the hotel bed, waiting for Donna and dwelling on the charms of the latest Sondheim musical, which had ended a scant hour before. His old nemesis the telephone, strangely silent during the few and scattered hours they'd spent in the hotel room during their Manhattan stay, began a soft, almost apologetic ringing. He reflected that a New York phone really should be shriller.

'Hello.'

'Jerry, this is Ab Kelley.' His old friend's voice was tired and subdued.

223

'Hi, Ab. What's up?'

'I've been up too long. I've been trying to reach you for hours. Jerry, we want you to do the TV call on tomorrow's broadcast. I'll have a fresh contract for you to sign in the morning. OK?'

'But, Ab, what about Grant Engle?'

'You haven't heard? Where have you been?'

'In the park with George.'

'George? I thought you brought Donna with you.'

'Never mind. What haven't I heard about?'

'Engle. He's dead. They found him in the parking lot out at Belmont this afternoon, strangled.'

★   ★   ★

'At least you can be thankful you didn't find the body this time,' Donna pointed out. 'You were nowhere near Belmont Park and you can prove it.'

'Donna,' Jerry assured her, 'I was never a serious suspect.'

'You looked like one in that news clip I saw from Baltimore. And when they say you aren't a suspect that's TV shorthand that you are a suspect.'

'Don't be silly.'

'And, anyway, this time you have a real

224

motive.'

'Motive?'

'Sure. With Grant Engle out of the way, you get to call the race on national TV.'

'That can't be enough of a motive.'

'It can for a maniac.'

'Do I look like a maniac to you?'

She slid her arm under the covers and stroked his chest. 'It's not what you look like to me, Jerry. I'm just glad you're out of it this time. Can't we try to get a little sleep or something?'

'They'll be coming to question us.'

'What you mean *us*, Kemo Sabay? Anyway, I'm sure they'll let it wait until tomorrow.'

Jerry wished they wouldn't. There were so many things he wanted to know. Who of the group from Masterton's party and the Hotel Sorenson in Baltimore had been (or could have been) in close enough proximity to the Belmont parking lot to have killed Engle? And had he had a red rose on his body like the others? Jerry was sure he must have, but that aspect of the case still had not become public knowledge, and the New York police were sure to keep it under their hats.

'This proves I'm right, Donna.'

'Right on what?'

'It's all connected to the Masterton farm and the gelding of Blueskying. Engle was the only person left in the case who was there at the time of the incident, and now he's dead. It has nothing to do with who owns the favorite. Martin Fine can stop quaking in his boots.'

'Unless the killing of Engle is unconnected to the others.'

'That seems unlikely.'

'Unlikeliness doesn't seem to be a barrier. Let's go to sleep, Brogan. I've finally reached the point where I think I can sleep in New York.'

'Somehow I'm not sleepy.'

'Let me see if I can help make you sleepy.'

'What are you going to do? Throw sand in my eyes? Hit me with a mallet? Bring in a herd of sheep?'

'I'm going to take your mind off Old Rosebud.'

BELMONT 2

The next morning, Jerry and Donna were joined at breakfast in the hotel coffee-shop by Ab Kelley, who looked tired and drawn and nearly as harried as he'd sounded on the phone the night before. He offered some papers for Jerry's signature, and Jerry discovered to his surprise just how much monetary difference there was between working for network radio and working for network television.

'I know this is an artistic drop in class,' he said, 'but I think I can handle it.'

Ab smiled wanly. 'Has anybody from the police been around to talk to you yet?'

'No,' Jerry said shortly.

'He feels left out,' Donna said.

'You won't be for long. I think you'll hear from them this morning. I hope they'll leave us alone at the track this afternoon. Doing a broadcast is tough enough without getting the third degree during the commercials.'

'Have they connected Engle's death with the other crimes?' Jerry asked.

'If they haven't, there are plenty of people to do it for them.' He produced a morning paper with the glaring headline 'Old Rosebud Killer Takes Third Victim' and passed it across to Jerry.

Details were sparse. Engle's body had been found a couple of hours after the conclusion of the day's races. How long he had been there in the parking lot, or who had found him, was vague. One question was answered, though: the police were no longer trying to keep Old Rosebud's calling card a secret. A single red rose *had* been found on the body, and the connection had been made to the killings of

Van Ness Masterton and Bettina Winslow.

In a sidebar story, Martin Fine managed to express both horror and relief at Engle's death. But the reporter had scrounged up some additional speculative quotes, not from police sources, to suggest the favorite's owner might not be completely out of the woods until the current year's Belmont was history.

'The paper doesn't mention the people who were at the scene of both other murders. I hope the police have explored that. It could help them,' said Jerry.

'Not much. Most of the rest of us were at the races yesterday, while you were at Grant's Tomb or wherever the hell you were.'

'Ab, you're just jealous because I dropped out of the circle of suspects.'

'It's a good thing. This time you had a motive.'

'Me?'

'That's what I tried to tell him,' Donna said.

Jerry said with mock pomposity, 'Shouldn't *I* be the authority on whether or not I had a motive? OK, OK, you got me. I confess. Actually, I killed Masterton and Bettina just as a smokescreen. Engle was the man I was really after.' He gestured to his contract. 'With this extra money, I can eat in New York's best restaurants for a day and a half if I skip breakfast. Knowing I would be the chief suspect, I cleverly provided myself with a perfect alibi.'

Donna said, 'That's the first time I've ever been accused of perfection.'

'The hell it is. While you were admiring the view from the top of the Empire State Building yesterday afternoon, I slipped away, ostensibly to buy my Aunt Olivia a postcard, went down the elevator to the ground floor, hurried to the nearest subway station where I used my newfound expertise on the New York transportation system to get to Penn Station, got on the Long Island Railroad special to Belmont, killed Engle, retraced my steps, and rejoined you before you had even spotted the UN building.'

'That's a pretty tight schedule.'

'I know, but I took the express elevator.' Jerry sighed. 'We shouldn't be joking about this, I suppose. I didn't like Engle, but he probably deserved to live a little longer.'

Ab shrugged. 'Why be hypocritical about it? I'm not mourning the guy.'

'Who was there on the scene, of the people who were at the Masterton party?'

'Well, let's see. Bill and Arleen Holman were there. Emmett Winslow was there. He finally decided to scratch Pepperpot from the Belmont, but he was running another one of

229

his horses in the stake yesterday and wasn't going to leave town until today. I saw Les Randall in the pressbox. The widow Masterton was around, and her trainer Nurock, of course. Acton Schoolcraft was there, too. I think that's all that I know of.'

'Have the police been able to eliminate any of them?'

'They don't confide in me. You'll have a chance to ask them first hand, though, in no time at all.'

'Did you talk to Engle at all yesterday before he died?'

'No, but we had a splendid chat after he died.'

'Ab, be serious. Did he seem worried earlier in the day?'

'No more so than usual. That guy has been erratic as hell and drunk half the time ever since the first killing. Yesterday was no exception. But he wouldn't let me in on what he was worried about. Sometimes he'd use miscalling the Derby winner for an excuse, but he didn't convince me.'

'Right. That wasn't it at all. From the time of Masterton's death, he'd had reason to fear for his life. The fear was intensified after Bettina was killed. The mistake at Churchill Downs had nothing to do with it. What was he like before the last few weeks, Ab? Did you always have to worry about his drinking?'

'No. That's what was funny about it. I never thought much of Grant Engle as a broadcaster or as a man, Jerry, but he was never a drunk. In fact, he had a sort of mediocre reliability about him, at least professionally. He had a great voice, but he wasn't good enough at his job to be an erratic drunk over a long period of time. His trouble all started after the Derby.'

'I know when it really started. Almost to the minute. When Bettina Winslow showed me one of her Old Rosebud messages and I pointed out it was full of the names of geldings, she was shocked as hell, though she tried to conceal it. And what was the first thing she did after that? She took Engle aside for some intense conversation. Why Engle? Because he was her latest extra-marital lover and confidant? Or because he was around at the time of the Blueskying incident and shared some guilty secret with her? I think Old Rosebud, whoever he is, had some revenge motive against Masterton and Bettina and Engle, and it had something to do with the mistaken gelding of Blueskying.'

'What do you think it was?'

'I don't know. But something. And it had something to do with Denny Kilbride, a.k.a. Percy Mayo, too. I don't think his death was a

231

coincidence.'

'Did Old Rosebud kill him, too?'

'I don't know, but probably.'

'As a dry run, maybe.'

'There was no rose on the body, but he may have been saving that for his Triple Crown series. Ab, I'll bet you the Old Rosebud killer is finished. He's done his work. If he kills again, it can only be to cover his tracks. Why tie his series of murders in with the Triple Crown races if he has more than three of them in mind?'

'Maybe if they haven't caught him by then, he'll do an encore for the Travers.'

'You guys are sure funny,' Donna said gloomily. 'I don't know what the Travers is, but I don't really care much, either. Look, Jerry, I know vacation's over and today's a work day. But stick to the TV-radio work, will you?'

'Sure. Would I meddle where I'm not wanted?'

★   ★   ★

Each Triple Crown race had its advantages and drawbacks. In the case of the Belmont Stakes, the consensus of horsemen was that it was the greatest race of them all, with its testing distance of a mile and a half. But it didn't have the pageantry associated with the Kentucky Derby and the Preakness. Someone had said the Derby was the 'Run for the Roses', the Preakness was the 'Middle Jewel', but the Belmont was the 'seventh at New York'. The race did have its official traditions; a theme song, 'The Sidewalks of New York'; a flower, the carnation; an official drink, logically called the White Carnation; the Esposito's Fence, a neighboring tavern's picket fence which was always painted in the colors of the winning owner. But the Belmont traditions almost seemed like perfunctory gestures toward the festival-day glamor that came naturally to the Derby and the Preakness. Off-track betting had reduced the attendance at New York racetracks generally in recent years and, though the Belmont could still be relied upon to bring out a crowd, it seemed unlikely the throng of 82,694 that saw Pass Catcher win in 1971 would ever be approached again. The Belmont management could make one telling claim, however: theirs was the only Triple Crown race that saw no increase in admission prices over those for a regular racing day.

Throughout the clubhouse, grandstand and pressbox, horse people from throughout the United States and the world were waiting for the great moment to arrive. They didn't need pageantry.

'We should have stayed home,' said Bill Holman, looking down at Belmont Park's unique mile-and-a-half oval from a box seat near the finish line. 'It was just stupid to come here.'

'I know you don't always get along with my family, Bill,' Arleen began.

'It isn't that, honey. But we could have come back to see them any other time in the world but now. I wanted to go to a few more parties, get a few more free drinks, pretend I was a member of the jet set, and it's landed us in the middle of another police investigation. My pal Jerry Brogan seems to thrive on that kind of stuff, but I don't.'

'How were we to know there'd be another murder? Or that we'd be on the scene?' Arleen said comfortingly.

'It was a case of waiting for the other shoe to drop. The third shoe, in this case.'

'You're taking this too hard, Bill. It hasn't been so bad answering a few questions. We're not suspects. We didn't even know Grant Engle, and nothing we could have done would have prevented his death.'

'At least we had sense enough to leave Tall Sequoia at home. He missed the police interrogation and got his Lasix, too. If they didn't have such antiquated medication rules in this state, he'd have had a good shot at this race.'

'We could have run him if you'd planned to, but he's better off where he is. Anyway, I'm planning to enjoy this, whatever happens.' She opened her program to the field for the Belmont Stakes, three races away, and studied the illustrated colors of the seven entries.

★   ★   ★

Not far away was a woman with a more personal interest in the day's proceedings. Carol Masterton had sat distractedly through the fourth race, an overnight stake for promising three year olds who weren't quite ready for the Belmont. Her companion, Acton Schoolcraft, had watched the race with interest through his binoculars. When it was over, he said, 'It's a poor crop of threes this year, Carol. Not a truly distinguished runner in the bunch. Except maybe Gotham City, of course.'

'Maybe? There was no maybe about it a few weeks ago.'

'Things change quickly in the world of the turf, my dear. I think we have a good offer.'

That morning Acton had given her the latest proposed syndication figure, contingent on an impressive Belmont win by Gotham City. By any sane standard, the figure seemed absurdly high, but in comparison with other recent syndications of classics winners it sounded somewhat paltry. Subtract a couple more million, and the figure would be downright insulting.

'I don't want to do it, Acton.'

'It would be a shame to take such a loss on Van's other holdings when a little more capital from you could—'

'I'm not interested in those other businesses, Acton. I can just sell them off and concentrate on horses.'

With a raspy chuckle, Schoolcraft said, 'You'd lose millions, Carol, maybe tens of millions.'

She shook her head. 'What does it mean? It's all out of perspective. I could lose tens of millions and still have enough left over for any normal person to retire on twenty times over. What do I want with more money than I can use, Acton?'

Schoolcraft only shook his head, as if the answer were such an obvious one it was beyond the need or the possibility of explanation.

★   ★   ★

The seat Jerry had acquired for Donna was a good one, but before half the Belmont card had been run she had a better one. Martin Fine invited her to the Garden Terrace on the fourth floor of the clubhouse, to watch the races with him from his heavily secured goldfish bowl. Seemingly over his Old Rosebud jitters, he confidently evicted one of his bodyguards. At first Donna was upset at causing the bodyguard to lose his seat, but when a wink told her the guy would welcome getting away from the TV star for a while she accepted.

'No, I'm not afraid of getting killed any more,' Fine told her. 'Not really, or I wouldn't place you in jeopardy. I think it's one murder to a customer. I mean, one murder to a classic; of course, it's one murder to a customer. Anyhow, you're safe here with me.'

'Sure, I know that,' she said.

'Yeah, you know that. That's my whole image. If I were Tom Selleck, would you feel safe with me?'

She grinned. 'No, but I still might not mind.'

Glancing appreciatively at Donna's legs, Fine said, 'Just be glad you wore a dress instead of jeans or you couldn't even sit up here. Not even in designer jeans. And I couldn't sit here without a jacket. There's still a lot of East Coast in me, but dress codes are hard for my California half to take. Still, it could be worse. They could demand a tie.'

As the races went on, she gave him a résumé of the three plays she and Jerry had watched for the last three nights. Fine seemed to appreciate her professional drama teacher's eye for stagecraft, and the conversation served to calm the actor down, take his mind at least fleetingly off the performance of his colt in the Belmont. The more Donna got to know Fine, the less she was bothered by the intense nervous energy that fueled him. Maybe she was getting used to him, or maybe release from an imagined sentence of death had mellowed him somewhat.

Either way, she would enjoy the afternoon.

★　　　★　　　★

Before he entered the TV booth to prepare for his call of the Belmont, Jerry had a brief and unexpected visitor. It was Baltimore's Detective Sutherland.

'You *did* make it,' Jerry said cordially.

'Yeah, I worked it out. I made a terrific speech in support of police co-operation, pointing out the uniquely interdepartmental nature of this series of crimes and the necessity for unprecedented measures to deal with them. So here I am.'

'Is Morton from Lexington here, too?'

'No, he doesn't like the races. What do you know, Mr Brogan?'

'About what? I've sworn off amateur detective work. Your Big Apple colleagues didn't like my theory any better than you did.'

'It is a bit fragmentary, you must admit. At least you gave me a winner.'

'Tall Sequoia? I got lucky.'

'No, no, a *Belmont* winner. Collate. Remember?'

'Oh, yeah. My Belmont system. Well, just remember, nobody can be right every time.'

'But no racing insider would give somebody a guaranteed winner if he wasn't sure, would he?'

That could not be a threatening look in Sutherland's eye, Jerry assured himself. It was all in his imagination. Still, he hoped the Baltimore cop hadn't put too much of his hard-earned money on Collate.

Oddly enough, Jerry's better-paid and ostensibly more important position as TV commentator actually involved less work than the radio assignment. He missed the extra duties, since he didn't really need more time for jitters or (he was beginning to think) more time to throw the circumstances of the Old

239

Rosebud murders around in a brain that seemed able to juggle them endlessly without a pattern emerging. His brief interview with the New York police detectives had added nothing to his knowledge, nor, he considered, to theirs.

Another announcer had been brought in to do the radio color, television performers being too important to bother with such details. Both radio and TV would now use Jerry's account of the race. Jerry's one responsibility aside from the call itself would be to participate in a straw poll among the TV broadcast team as to which horse would win. While Jerry had been handling the radio coverage of the Derby and the Preakness as a team of one, he was part of an overstocked roster of six working on the Belmont telecast: a star sports anchor who knew baseball and basketball inside out and had a vague understanding of the difference between a horse and a cow; a former Miss America who smiled prettily and did lightweight 'human interest' reports; a knowledgeable and articulate ex-jockey who had the most to say and the least chance to say it; a female exercise rider turned broadcaster who had the thankless (and rather pointless) task of trying to interview the jockeys from horseback both on the way to the post and after the race had been run; and of course the inevitable Artie (the Line) Prince.

Jerry watched his monitor, suffering through the inanities he'd been able to avoid when concentrating on radio. Artie the Line was assuring his audience, 'Valid Point liked those sharp Pimlico turns, where he got second, but he doesn't want this long a distance. And his jockey's not used to the special problems of a mile-and-a-half oval like we have here at Belmont. Doc Paul is the favorite, owned by my buddy Marty Fine, a great actor and a great guy, but he won't be the same horse in the East he was out in California. There's something about California. Tall Sequoia had everything his way in the Preakness, but they were wise to take him back home and save him the disgrace of losing the Belmont. Penticton, the Canadian horse, will like the long distance, but I don't think he has the class of the rest of these. The best runners from north of the border come from the eastern provinces, not out there in British Columbia. Collate is green as the money his new owners shelled out for him, and I don't think he's ready for this kind of a test yet. Fortuitous I really don't like. He can't be trusted. Financial Whiz is a hot horse, but sometimes you gotta be suspicious of hot horses. Gotham City is trying for a comeback. They say he was real upset by the passing of his owner, Van Ness Masterton—a good friend of mine and a great guy, by the way—but now he's over it. He's fresh. He knows this track, and he knows these fans. His jockey's won three races here already today. He's lost two in a row and he doesn't want to lose again. Gotham City's my pick.'

Following Artie's outpouring of irrelevancies, the star anchor picked Doc Paul; Miss America, noted for her hard-nosed business sense, picked Financial Whiz; the former jockey tabbed Penticton; the horseback interviewer seconded Gotham City; and finally Jerry was asked for his selection. He didn't know if the race-caller, a symbol of integrity or anyway objectivity, should really offer one, but this was how it was done on TV, or anyway the present network. He'd have preferred to champion a colt no one else had mentioned (perhaps Collate, though he assured himself Detective Sutherland of Baltimore would be too busy with other things to be monitoring his TV performance), but having seen Doc Paul's breathtaking run at Hollywood Park he had to go along with Martin Fine's colt.

The telecast went to commercial, and the seven entries drew nearer the starting gate.

'Want me to send a bet for you?' Martin Fine asked. He had just returned from the walking ring with his unaccustomed entourage. He needed them today to protect him from the media and the public, regardless of Old Rosebud's intentions.

Donna grinned and fished two dollars from her purse. 'Doc Paul across the board.'

The actor smiled. 'It takes six dollars to bet across the board.'

'Oh. To place, then.'

'Not to win?' He mocked disappointment.

'Nope,' she said. 'No reflection on Doc Paul, but I'm a very conservative bettor.' She had been ever since her first losing win bet.

'As you wish, Madam,' he said, and sent a network flunky to place the bet. Donna wasn't too comfortable with that, but maybe this guy wanted to get away for a while, too.

'Do you and Jerry have plans for after the race?' Fine asked.

'No, not that I know of. And I guess I would.'

'I'm staying in a penthouse apartment on Park Avenue. One of the network honchos who's in Europe now lives there, and they arranged for me to have it for the week. Much easier and quieter and safer than staying in a hotel. It's a gorgeous place. You'll love it. Guy's an art collector, and he's got some stuff you wouldn't believe. Makes me want to do a show on art collecting—not art fraud, we did art fraud our third year. Anyway, what I'm getting around to is why don't you two come up for a drink and a little relaxation after the races? I'd be honored. If there's anything else you want to do later on, there'll be plenty of time. New York's a small town as far as travel time is concerned.'

'That sounds very nice to me,' Donna said.

'Terrific. Look, the security plans call for me to get out of here as quick as possible after the Belmont is run. After the winner's circle ceremony, I hope. I don't know our exact route or anything. I suspect I'll have to talk to reporters somewhere along the way, but I'll keep it short.' Martin produced a tattered sheet of paper from his jacket pocket. 'Why don't I send Jerry up a message to join us at my place later? I'll write him a note on this press handout on Old Rosebud. That'll give him a laugh.'

Donna hesitated. But Jerry had promised earlier to do anything she wanted tonight, and they didn't have to stay at the actor's apartment long if Jerry didn't want to. She knew he liked Fine anyway. 'All right,' she said. 'That'll be great.'

★   ★   ★

The seven colts approaching the Belmont starting gate all looked like winners, Jerry decided. Their coats were glossy, their conformation unexceptionable, their legs devoid of the scars and bandages that sometimes marked lesser animals. Throughout the post parade, Financial Whiz had seemed the liveliest, prancing on his toes with ears pricked. Gotham City was almost sleepy-looking, which may not have been a good sign. The bettors displayed an unprecedented coolness toward the appropriately named local hero. For the first time in a New York start (or any other), Gotham City was not the favorite. He was third choice at 7–2 behind Doc Paul (9–5) and Financial Whiz (5–2). Penticton was offered at 9–2, with Collate 8–1, Valid Point 10–1, and Fortuitous the longshot of the field at 15–1.

The TV camera took one last look at Martin Fine, intensely waiting for the start. Jerry had been surprised the first time he'd looked at his monitor and seen Donna sitting next to Fine, but he knew both of them too well to regard the actor as a rival. He planned to kid her about it later, though: 'Anything to get on TV, huh, Melendez?' All over America, people would be trying to guess the beautiful Chicana's identity. And it should cause a sensation at Richard Henry Dana High.

The seven three year olds had the demeanor of old pros as they loaded into the starting gate, located just before the finish line in the middle of the Belmont Park stretch. Six of them entered without fuss and the seventh, Collate, only somewhat living up to his reputation for greenness, offered token reluctance.

The star anchor said, 'And now let's go to Jerry Brogan for the call of the Belmont Stakes!'

Though he'd been as calm as Gotham City up to now, it occurred to Jerry in a sudden flash of insight that the call he was about to make would be heard by more people than attended Surfside Meadows in an entire season of racing. The opening of the starting gate fortunately precluded any further statistical wheel-spinning.

'They're off! Financial Whiz goes for the lead, with Gotham City second, followed by Doc Paul, Penticton, Valid Point, Collate and Fortuitous.'

While the Derby and Preakness fields had included horses with intense early speed, this Belmont was one of those races where no one wanted the lead. The rider on Financial Whiz was practically standing up in the saddle to restrain his mount, but none of the others went by him to make the pace. This classic would be run European style with slow early fractions.

'Into the first turn, it's Financial Whiz in front by one length. Gotham City's second, also under a snug hold, by a head. Doc Paul is third on the outside by a half-length, followed by Collate, Valid Point, Penticton and Fortuitous. The first quarter, a very slow twenty-five and one. Turning for the backstretch, it's now Financial Whiz, with Gotham City coming to him between horses and Doc Paul staying with them on the outside in third. Then it's Valid Point and Collate, Penticton and Fortuitous.'

The first three were gradually stepping up the pace and leaving the other four several lengths behind. The half-mile time of fifty seconds flat was still agonizingly slow.

'Along the backstretch, approaching the halfway point, it's now Doc Paul taking the lead on the outside by a head. Gotham City stays with him second, and Financial Whiz drops back to third along the rail. It's three lengths back to Valid Point in fourth, followed by Collate, Penticton and Fortuitous.'

Jerry glanced at the infield tote-board timer for the six-furlong split. The three quarter had been fairly fast, but the aggregate of one minute and thirteen seconds was still plowhorse time.

Financial Whiz had dropped three lengths back into third now, with the Masterton colt and Martin Fine's charger still dueling for the lead. As the field entered the far turn, it was looking more and more like a two-horse race.

'Into the turn, it's Gotham City and Doc Paul head and head! Financial Whiz is third and the rest far out of it. They went the mile in one/thirty-five and four!' The fourth quarter had been an incredibly quick twenty-two and two. The two leaders were humming now, moving as one horse into the last half-mile of the race.

In the clubhouse, Donna tried to watch the race and ignore the fact that Martin Fine, who had thrown an impulsive arm around her when Doc Paul started his move on the backstretch, was squeezing her like a rag doll while shouting unheard encouragement at his colt. Carol Masterton, watching Gotham City, was silent, pale and tight-lipped. Acton Schoolcraft was watching her more intently than he was the horses.

'Turning into the stretch, it's now Doc Paul inching ahead on the outside, but Gotham City does not crack. He keeps coming back. It's eight lengths back to Financial Whiz in third, another four to Penticton, and the other three horses are far back. They're still head and head down the stretch, Gotham City and Doc Paul.'

From there to the finish, Jerry tried to discover how many different ways he could say the leaders were head and head with nothing between them. And that was the way they flashed under the line. 'Gotham City gets it by the shortest of noses from Doc Paul,' Jerry said and felt an immediate compulsion to hedge. 'It was a very, very close finish. Could easily be a dead heat. Penticton got up for third, and Financial Whiz was fourth.'

Martin Fine impulsively planted a kiss on Donna's cheek an instant after the finish. It was seen in millions of living rooms. 'I think he did it, Donna. Don't you think he did it?'

'It was very close,' Donna ventured.

Carol Masterton was asking Acton Schoolcraft the same question. The elderly billionaire shook his head, gazing at the time on the tote-board clock. 'Disappointing time,' he said. 'After that fourth quarter, they surely should have done better than two/twenty-eight and two. It's a weak crop of three year olds, Carol.'

She wasn't listening. Tears coursing down her cheeks, she said, 'He ran beautifully. Win or lose, he ran his heart out.'

'It's not what I hoped for, but we can still make a syndication deal if we act now. For a little less than I said, because I was looking for a much more impressive Belmont. Still, if he wins the photo. . .'

'If he wins or loses the photo, Acton, he's mine and I'm keeping him!'

Jerry's on-track teammate was again on horseback with her directional mike, getting the opinions of the two jockeys involved as to which had got there first. They agreed it was very, very close.

Arleen Holman, still thrilled by the close finish, had to ask. 'Bill, how would Tall Sequoia have done if we'd brought him back?'

Bill answered, honestly but ambiguously, 'It wouldn't even have been close.'

*　　*　　*

The photo showed that Artie (the Line) Prince had been right at the beginning of the race, and Jerry had been right at the end of it. Gotham City was again the toast of Gotham City. Both Carol Masterton, a gracious winner, and Martin Fine, a gracious loser, had been interviewed by breathless TV reporters. Another Triple Crown series was history.

'Terrific job, Jerry,' Ab Kelley was assuring him in the midst of a gabble of world and national press.

'Thanks,' said Jerry. He saw dozens of familiar faces among the gathered reporters. There was Miles Waters. Still on vacation from the London *Times*? There was something he'd wanted to ask Miles... No chance of getting to him now, though.

The figure of Detective Sutherland loomed up suddenly. Jerry was glad to see he was smiling.

'You didn't lose too much on Collate, I hope,' Jerry said with a weak grin.

'You gotta be kidding,' the Baltimore cop said. 'I had my bread on Gotham City. You didn't think I was going to believe that line of crap about winners that start with a C, did you?'

No resentment apparent. At least that was one less thing to worry about.

'This message came for you earlier,' Ab said. 'I would have got it to you sooner, but it's been a madhouse up here.'

Jerry looked at the printed side of the sheet first. 'What is this?'

'It's just a fact-sheet the track put out on Old Rosebud the horse. A lot of the reporters here wanted more information. The media relations people didn't really want to emphasize the murders, but this was something they could provide to be helpful, so

251

of course they did.'

'Of course.' The sheet gave the salient details about Old Rosebud, beginning with his breeding, by Uncle out of Ivory Bells by Himyar; his race record of eighty starts, forty wins, thirteen seconds and eight thirds; his total earnings of $74,729, impressive at the time but laughable now; his victories in great American races, some still on the calendar (the Kentucky Derby, Clark Handicap, Carter Handicap and Paumonok Handicap) and other nostalgic whispers of racing history (the US Hotel Stakes, the Cincinnati Trophy, and his first victory as a two year old, the Yucatan Stakes in Juarez, Mexico). Jerry was studying the sheet as if mesmerized.

'Jerry,' Ab pointed out, 'the message is on the other side. He was just using that as scratch paper.'

'Oh, sure.' Jerry turned the sheet over. A scrawled, friendly note from Martin Fine. He and Donna had gone on to his temporary penthouse apartment where they hoped Jerry would join them later. 'She hopes it more than I do, of course,' Martin had written. 'Seriously, Jerry, she's perfectly safe with me. On national TV.'

'We're having a big bash later at the Essex House,' Ab said. 'Will you kids be able to join us?'

'I hope so,' Jerry said distractedly, 'but I have something else to take care of first. I need to get a cab to an address on Park Avenue as soon as I can. But first, maybe I ought to. . .' Now Jerry looked Ab in the eye excitedly, like a man coming out of a daze. 'Ab, I know who Old Rosebud is. And I should have known a long time ago.'

POST-MORTEM

Martin Fine swung open the door of his temporary dwelling and gave Jerry a cordial clap on the shoulder.

'Glad you could come, Jerry, glad you could come. Come on in. Isn't this place terrific?'

Jerry looked around. Though his mind was too much on other things to take it all in, he gathered the television executive who owned the place was an unusually eclectic art collector. Greek and American Indian sculptures were side by side; Picasso and Jackson Pollock warred with Norman Rockwell and Grandma Moses. The furniture was all duck-down white. There was no TV set in sight.

'That's quite a gauntlet I had to run to get up here, Martin. Those guys downstairs are doing everything short of a strip search.'

'Aw, I'm sorry you had to go through that, Jerry.'

'No, no problem. It's a good thing really.'

'Part of it's special for me, but part of it's just New York. I couldn't live back here again, Jerry. People are too frantic.' Martin laughed. The joke on himself had been intentional, but Jerry didn't join him.

'You don't seem yourself, Jerry. Something bothering you?'

'No, no, it's nothing. Where's Donna?'

'Out looking at the view. It's beautiful, Jerry. Manhattan's great from a safe distance. Shall we join her?'

'Sure,' Jerry said. Fine opened a sliding door, and they stepped out onto the patio of the penthouse. The lights of New York glittered on all sides. Jerry saw Donna's slender form leaning against a wall that was low enough to see over but too high for accidental falls.

'Hi, Jerry,' she said. 'I collected a bet on Doc Paul today.'

'She had him to place,' Fine said. 'Smarter than I was.'

'That was a tough break, Martin,' Jerry said. 'Your colt almost did it.'

'Aw, I was proud of him. It took one terrific horse to beat him, and we'll be trying Gotham

City again later in the summer. He doesn't scare us. Maybe in the Travers. I've never been to Saratoga.'

'You don't see many as close as the race today. It reminded me of the Affirmed versus Alydar Belmont.'

The actor shrugged philosophically. 'So Doc Paul has gone from Secretariat to Alydar in a matter of a couple of weeks. We'll take all the compliments we can get. Can I fix you kids a drink?'

'That'd be great,' Jerry said. 'Just a beer for me, though.'

Donna handed the actor a glass perched on the edge of the wall and requested another of the same. Fine disappeared back into the penthouse.

'Jerry, isn't this terrific?' Donna said. 'I hope you don't mind my accepting Martin's invitation, but...'

'Donna, that's OK, that's fine, that's terrific,' Jerry said. 'Don't worry about that.'

She looked him in the eye with a touch of suspicion. 'What should I worry about, Brogan?'

'I've finally doped it out. I know who Old Rosebud is. It was staring me in the face all the time.'

'Who is it?'

Before Jerry could answer, Martin Fine

appeared with the drinks. 'It's getting a little chilly out here,' he said. 'Should we all go back inside?'

'Sure,' said Jerry.

The lobby intercom buzzed just as they stepped into the massive living room. Fine pushed a button on the wall and spoke into the air. 'Yeah?'

'Mr Fine, there's another guy wants to see you.'

'I'm not expecting anybody else.'

'Sure, I know, but I thought I ought to check. He's a pretty persistent character.'

'Who is he?'

'His name is Les Randall.'

Fine almost spat at the wall speaker. 'Goddam it, he's a reporter. You know I don't want to talk to any reporters. Especially that one.'

Jerry touched the actor's shoulder. 'Martin, let him come up.'

'What? Why? I got nothing to say to that bastard.'

'Let him come up. I have a good reason. Really.'

'OK, OK, let him come up,' Fine told the wall.

The actor turned back to his guests. He looked disgusted, but he strained to remain the cordial host. 'OK, so he's on his way. The

256

guy never surrenders, I'll say that for him. The one good thing is he may be so surprised I agreed to see him he'll have a heart attack and die on the elevator.'

Fine perched on the front few inches of a white easy chair. Jerry and Donna had sat on a long matching sofa. Jerry put a protective arm around her shoulder. She looked at him searchingly, wondering just exactly what was going on.

'Why, Jerry?' Fine asked. 'Huh? Why did you impose on my good nature to let that creep come up here?'

'I want to suggest an article to him.'

'Oh, great. Are we *all* gonna be on the front of the next *National Onlooker*?'

'I doubt it.'

'I'll string along with you, Jerry, because you're my pal,' Fine said. 'In a couple of hours, with a little luck, maybe you'll *still* be my pal.'

The doorbell rang, and Fine got up to let Les Randall into the apartment. 'Come on in, Les,' Fine said with satirical politeness. 'Glad to see you.'

'I say, this is good of you,' the journalist said. 'I knew you wouldn't blackball a chap forever just for doing his job.'

'Certainly not. Come and have a seat. Have a drink? The beer is all cold, but I could put some in the microwave.'

Randall forced a laugh. 'Very amusing. Vodka and lime if you have it. Well, hello, Jerry, this is a surprise, and—' He spotted Donna. 'Why, isn't this remarkable? I do believe I have the exclusive of a lifetime.'

'This is Donna Melendez,' said Jerry. 'Donna. Les Randall.'

'How do you do?' said Donna. 'I've heard so much about you.'

'Quite so,' said Randall. 'I knew the old ears were burning about something.'

Fine brought Randall's drink, and the four of them sat down. They were an uneasy quartet, to put it mildly.

'Well, Les,' said Martin Fine, 'before you ask your first question, let me clear the air. Everybody knows now that your last article on me, where you did your best to make me out a sniveling coward and ruin my career forever, was a crock of shit. And I'm too big for a twerp like you to ruin anyway. So as the odor fades I won't say another word about that.'

'I say, so that's what you call clearing the air.' Randall didn't seem fazed.

'Now, as to your question about Ms Melendez, she is a friend of mine and a friend of Mr Brogan's whom I asked to join me for a few races today while Mr Brogan was working. We are not an item for your lousy paper, and anything you write that goes the slightest bit over the legal edge will precipitate a libel suit, certainly from me and maybe from her, too. Let me add that, while I may be a public figure for purposes of your crummy yellow journalism, she's not. I continue to be a happily married working stiff whose wife just happens not to care for the public eye, and I think she has more of a point every day. And that's all I've got to say on *that* subject.'

'The air gets clearer and clearer.'

'Now, the reason you're up here is that Mr Brogan, not me, wanted to talk to you. Jerry, the floor is yours.'

So it was. Jerry gave Donna's hand a squeeze and looked at the two faces across the glass coffee-table. Had this been a good idea? He wasn't sure, but it was too late to turn back now.

'Les, I have an idea for you. I think you should do an in-depth article on the Old Rosebud killer, something more searching and substantial than anyone has done up to now. I think the death of Grant Engle was the end of his string, that he's now done what he wanted to do. All that's left is an explanation of why he did it. People should understand that the reasons he committed those murders were good reasons. If people knew the whole story, they would sympathize with him. Don't you think so?'

'I haven't the foggiest whether they would or not. But, Jerry, you're talking about a journalist's dream of nirvana. If you can tell me how to get that story, of course, I would be more than interested. And very grateful as well.'

Jerry was silent for a moment. No one else spoke. He heard himself gulp. What was he getting himself into here?

'Let's hear it, Jerry,' said Martin Fine. 'You've got us all hooked.'

'It took me a long time to figure out who Old Rosebud was. Too long really. I guess the story starts with Denny Kilbride, an old trainer who went over the cliff at Surfside Beach. His real name was Percy Mayo, and he'd worked for Van Ness Masterton at the time the colt Bluesking was gelded by mistake. It may or may not have been Denny's fault, but he was blamed for it. He managed to get himself going again to a certain extent, becoming a trainer in California, even developing a good stakes horse. But he was a miserable, ruined man. Something happened to him a lot more terrible than just making a mistake or being blamed for one he didn't make. I don't know how Denny died, but I think now it was probably suicide. And I think the three Triple Crown crimes were committed on Denny's behalf. By somebody who cared about him and who was angered by the way he'd been treated after the Blueskying incident. Who wanted to get revenge on Masterton and the others who had ruined him. Maybe a relative of Denny's. Maybe a son. That much is just guesswork. But the identity of Old Rosebud is more than guesswork. I don't think I have any proof that would stand up in a court of law, but it's plenty to satisfy my own curiosity.

'I think the whole story would make the ultimate *National Onlooker* piece, Les. And though the reasons for what he did are understandable, by standards of the law, the Old Rosebud killer is probably insane. He would surely escape death and might even escape prison for that reason, especially if the public had a chance to learn his motive.'

Les Randall said, 'Keep talking, Jerry. I don't even have a good headline yet.'

'Why don't you drop the accent, Les?'

The journalist stared back at him. 'I daren't drop it, old boy. It might break.'

'It'd be a great story, Les. A first-person account of the Old Rosebud murders, written by Old Rosebud himself. How about it? Want to try it out on us?'

Randall leaned back in his chair, maintaining an icy calm somehow.

261

Fine was leaning forward, his eyes darting back and forth between the two of them. 'Don't try anything, Randall.'

'He won't,' Jerry said. 'He couldn't get past the bunch downstairs with any kind of weapon, and you and I can easily overpower him physically if we have to. Ready to talk about it, Les?'

'I'm more interested in why you believe I'm Old Rosebud, Jerry.'

'There were several indications, strong ones, though they didn't come together as fast as they should have. First of all, you're a phony Englishman. We all should have realized your "pip, pip, tally ho" line of speech was too much of a caricature to be real.'

'You'd be surprised, old boy. You hear it in the best London clubs.'

'At the Alibi Breakfast in Pimlico, I was sitting with one of your fellow London journalists, a *Times* writer who was obviously mortified at the image you were projecting. And as we parted he said something like, "We'll forgive you". At the time, I wasn't sure what he was talking about. I saw him again this afternoon before I left Belmont to come here, and I asked him what he'd meant by his remark. At first he didn't remember and asked me for the context. Then he caught on and assured me he was only joking. He wasn't really blaming me for Les Randall or even blaming America for him. He said weeds like that spring up in the best-kept gardens. I pressed him, to make sure I had it right. He'd meant he forgave America for sending Britain such an embarrassing asshole. He meant you were an American. My friend says everyone in Fleet Street knows you as an American, though you choose to pretend otherwise. He told me you've only been working for your paper about ten or twelve years, though your journalistic rise has been irritatingly swift. We both agreed you're a gifted fellow, Les. You soaked up their accent like a chameleon, acquired an encyclopedic knowledge of their racing history, and seemed in perfect tune with what my friend called "the attitudes and requirements of our working-class rags". As time went by, you started coming across more English than the English.'

'Really, Jerry, you're making heavy weather of a rather minor point,' said Les, not altering his silly-ass accent a whit. 'Even if I *had* changed my national identity for a culture I found more *sympatico*, that's hardly a hanging offense—now, is it?'

'No, Les. But that wasn't the main clue, just a supporting indicator. You were Old Rosebud, and I know it because you told me so. Quite deliberately.'

'Did I really? Oh, I say.' The drawing-room-comedy manner was becoming even more pronounced.

'Did you want to be caught, Les? Did you want to be stopped from committing more murders, or did you just get a kick out of skating on thin ice? Which was it?'

'You tell me, Sexton Blake.'

'Once I asked you how you got the way you are. I asked it with no particular purpose—I think I was just trying to be offensive because I found you such a pain in the ass. You made a reference to your family. "My father was my uncle," you said. "My mother's family made chimes from elephant tusks." If I were the kind of horseman who had an index file of equine family trees in my head, I'd have remembered that the original Old Rosebud was by a stud named Uncle out of a mare named Ivory Bells. But that kind of information goes out of my memory like flour through a sieve. I couldn't remember Secretariat's breeding without looking it up. This afternoon, I saw the information by chance on that press handout Martin used for scratch paper and it hit me like a ton of bricks. You were really having fun with me, weren't you, Les? But you've been having a ball through this whole thing, playing your little games, haven't you?'

'I say, old man,' Les said to Martin Fine, 'this is proving a most entertaining evening. We must get together like this more often. Maybe I was having fun telling you lies, Jerry. Maybe I thought it would be amusing to identify myself with Old Rosebud just to see if you were enough of an expert on your own country's racing to get the allusion. How about that?'

Jerry shook his head. 'That's not all, Les. I may have missed them before, but there were indicators from the very beginning that you were the most likely killer. Not just poison-pen writer but killer.

'My basic theory of this case, which has been scoffed at by police from coast to coast, was that there was one item missing from Masterton's carefully worked-out party game on the Triple Crown winners: the item that would represent Affirmed. I further theorized a court report in which an appellate court had affirmed a lower court's decision would be the most likely missing item, and in fact Donna here helped me find one that had a connection with the Blueskying incident, a federal case called *Cranstone Bloodstock Company versus Hopper*. To me the very existence of such a case proved my theory. For it *not* to be the missing item would be just too incredible a coincidence. No one agreed with me, though I think they will now. But, if my theory was correct, there was another question: was it likely that *Masterton* would have produced the account of a painful piece of litigation, one that reminded him of an incident he'd rather forget, to be part of his annual trivia game? The implication I drew was that *somebody else* chose the case report, somebody who helped him to gather the exhibits, somebody who had an unknown connection to the gelding business and who produced the report to show Masterton before he killed him so that the prospective victim would understand the motive for the murder before it took place. Then of course this second person had to carry it away with him to conceal the connection from investigators.

'But who had helped Masterton? Morton's investigation seemed to show no one had helped him plan the game, and if someone had done so innocently there would have been no reason not to say so. Then it occurred to me there was at least one person who spent time with Masterton the week before the party, an outsider who *could* have helped him work out the puzzle without someone in his household or anyone else knowing: journalist Les Randall. There was another little slip, Les. When you and I were talking to Masterton that night and he mentioned the coming game, you pretended you didn't know what he was talking about. You acted as if you thought you were going to be forced to watch a football game on TV. You had to have been lying, Les. The traditional party game was well known in racing society, and anyone who researched his subjects as thoroughly as you do would have to have known about it. Why would you conceal your knowledge without a reason?'

'Maybe I was just trying to be clever again,' said Les. 'I say, is this impressing anyone?' He looked challengingly at Martin Fine and at Donna. Silence greeted his question. Perhaps it was. 'You've said yourself, Jerry, none of this could hold up in a court of law.'

'That you're even talking about that means I'm getting through to you, Les. No, this won't stand up in court, but maybe other things will, once the police know where to look. You can't have covered your tracks everywhere. What about the computer printer you turned out the Old Rosebud letters on? Do you still have it somewhere, where the police experts can have a crack at identifying it? Or, better yet, did you get rid of it somewhere along the line? Sell it? Give it away? Hide it? I think the police can find it. Or what about the floppy disks you wrote the letters on? We know you reused some of them, so you must have stored the messages. Did you erase the disks? Or maybe you forgot to do that, eh, Les? What about it?'

The journalist gazed at Jerry with an expression that was hard to read. There was some amusement in it and some admiration but, overlaying everything else, a sudden weariness as well.

'I wish I could make you all understand,' he said.

'We want to understand, Les,' Jerry assured him, 'Don't we?' He appealed to Donna and Martin, who both nodded mute encouragement. 'Tell us about it.'

'I don't think I'll be writing it up for the *National Onlooker*, if you don't mind. You might enjoy this, though, Martin. It might make a script for that abominable television program of yours. And I promise I won't even sue you for libel.'

For once, the actor was silent.

Les Randall shrugged, 'Where to begin? I'm a journalist without a lead.'

'What's your real name, Les?' Jerry asked.

'You know, I'm never sure. But originally it was Lester Mayo. Then later it was Lester Fountain, after my mother's second husband.'

'You didn't grow up with your father?'

'No. No, I didn't. But I loved my father,

Jerry, I must tell you about him. He's the real story here, not Old Rosebud, not me. My father was a very gifted man, a man who knew horses like no one I've ever seen. Van Ness Masterton knew what he was doing when he hired him as farm manager. He wouldn't take an incompetent and put him in charge of one of the greatest collections of thoroughbred bloodstock in the world. The pressure of the job was hard on my father, but he could handle it. My parents' marriage couldn't, however, and they split up when I was very young. I lived with my mother and saw little of my father while growing up, and when she married a man named Fountain I was even obliged to take his name for a while. Probably I built my real father up into more of a heroic figure than he merited. Children do that.

'The Mastertons and Grant Engle were a threesome in those days, a drunken, carousing, revolting threesome that liked to play with people's lives over their martinis or mint juleps or whatever the hell they drank. Their first crime was breaking up my parents' marriage, but I suppose that was rather indirect. For a long time, they made it difficult for my father—just having to deal with that crowd was difficult at the best of times—but at least they treated him with a certain grudging respect, because they knew

269

an expert when they saw one. But when he made one mistake—and it was just a misunderstanding, a crazy accident that really wasn't his fault—they turned on him and destroyed him the way you'd kill a fly. He did surprisingly well afterward actually, tried to rebuild his life as a trainer on the leaky-roof circuit. At the time of his death he was on the fringe of the big time, but only on the fringe. He wasn't the same man, but he was existing. But they weren't through with him. He was an imperfect man, my father, but he didn't deserve what they did to him.'

Up to now, the cultured English accent had remained in place, and Randall had seemed calm and rational. But now, as he spoke about his grievance, the accent gradually began to slip, and with it Randall's control. 'My mother died before the Blueskying thing took place. I was finishing college at the time. I was a journalism major and an Anglophile, and my father's experiences, which I practically forced out of him in the hope that talking would do him some good, which I don't think it did. . . What the hell was I saying? Oh, yes, what happened to my father soured me on American racing and America generally. I went to Britain and wound up in Fleet Street. I did my best to become born-again British.'

'You did a good job,' said Donna quietly.

'Yes, I did, didn't I? Thank you for that. I did a damned good job, whatever that staid old hen from the bloody *Times* might have to say.' Now Randall was shifting back and forth between his affected English drawl and the harsher American intonations, and the look in his eye was becoming wilder. The three of them were starting to see the maniac Old Rosebud sitting before them.

'I made a nice living and a name for myself. I wasn't liked, but I didn't want to be liked. I wanted to be successful. Then came the opportunity to come back to America for a series of articles on American racing. It sounded like a lark, a giggle. But suddenly I found myself thrown among the very people who were responsible for my father's disgrace and ruin.'

Hatred glowed in Randall's eyes as he described them. 'Van Ness Masterton, that calm and reasonable equine businessman. Bettina Masterton, now Winslow, his perniciously fun-loving wife. Grant Engle, their former hanger-on, whose role in the Masterton stock farm's books and beds I never have quite figured out. They were such a fine group of people! Their deaths are such a loss to the world!'

'So you decided to take the opportunity to pick them off one by one,' Jerry said.

'Not at first!' Randall countered. The point seemed to be important to him. 'At the beginning, when I began sending the Old Rosebud letters, it was all a fantasy, the kind of precariously imperfect crime that a Walter Mitty might have plotted. I don't think I really meant or expected to go through with any of it.'

'Really, Les? It seemed so well planned.'

'Oh, it was planned in its way. But it depended on luck, too.'

Randall gave a sudden and very loud shout of laughter that echoed through the apartment and caused his three listeners to shiver.

'The idea of creating a crazy serial killer appealed to me no end, you know. I enjoyed the nutty ritual of it all, the threatening letters, the rose trademark, all that kitsch, and I also thought it might put investigators off looking for comprehensible motive.'

'That's why you sent the letters to everybody who had hopefuls for the classics, not just the ones you had targeted for death, right?'

'Oh, yes, Jerry, quite right. And Engle, being a commentator, didn't even qualify for any letters. Just for the rose, eh?'

'Your father had a letter in his pocket when he was found. You even sent him one?'

'I had to, since he had somehow come up

272

with a minor classics contender. A very minor one as it turned out. I went to see him—I hadn't for years—to explain to him what I was doing. He had no idea I'd become a Fleet Street journalist, and I hoped it would make him proud.'

'Didn't it?' Jerry asked.

'I don't think he'd ever heard of Fleet Street. At first, he seemed happy to see me, I must say. But when I revealed I was the author of the Old Rosebud letters his reaction shocked me. He screamed at me, said I was mad, said that for all his other sins he'd planted his seed to make a monster. Then he calmed down a bit and tried to tell me I needed help. That was worse. That hurt me terribly. Why should he react that way? It was just another sign of what they had made of him, what they had done to him. The next I knew he'd gone over the cliff at Surfside.'

'Then, you did kill him?' Jerry said.

'No, damn it! I wouldn't have done anything to hurt him. Do you imagine I'd kill my own father? The purpose was to save him, not to kill him. I wasn't there when he died. If I'd been there, I could have saved him.'

'It was suicide, then?'

'You may call it suicide, but I call it murder. *They* killed him. Van Ness Masterton. Bettina Winslow. Grant Engle.

When he died, I knew I had to go through with the Old Rosebud murders in earnest. Up to that time, as I've said, they were mainly a fantasy. Now they had truly robbed my father of everything, even his life, and I had to avenge him. I had no choice now. You have to see that.

'You know, I actually did have a bit of a Hamlet complex. For had I stayed on at the farm, if my parents had stayed married, if things had run their logical course, would I not have thought of Van Ness Masterton as my uncle? Wouldn't I have called him Uncle Van? And when my uncle killed my father I must take revenge on my uncle. I *was* Old Rosebud then, wasn't I, Jerry? I chose a good pseudonym there, didn't I?

'The particular fact of Old Rosebud having been a gelding was also a clue to my motive, and not an entirely unconscious one, but I doubted anyone would pick up on it. When I managed to gain an invitation to Masterton's party, I was able to convince him to make me a silent partner in his little party game, which served to cloud the issue nicely, of course. It may seem unlikely he would have let me help him, dear old Uncle Van, but we really had a very similar games-playing mentality, and he appreciated my quickness of wit and my breadth of knowledge. I suggested most of the exhibits, you see. I flatter myself that Masterton alone would have come up with something far more pedestrian. I wanted to use that one case report as a dramatic means of showing him before I killed him just who I was and why I was doing it. What a marvelous opportunity!'

'But you had to take the case report away with you,' Jerry said. 'You didn't want, especially so early in the going, to leave something behind that might make investigators think along lines you would prefer to have obscured.'

'Of course, you're right. But it was easily done. I was fairly sure I wouldn't be searched among all those bluebloods, and I was not, leaving a neat little puzzle I was convinced would confound the police. And I believe it did, didn't it? You never could convince them, could you, Jerry?'

'No,' Jerry breathed. 'I couldn't.'

'Don't feel badly about it,' Randall said consolingly. 'They don't live in the same world we do, Jerry.'

That gave Jerry his strongest shiver of horror of the whole evening. 'Tell us about Baltimore,' he prompted.

'More good luck. That so many of the guests from the Masterton party were all staying in the same hotel was quite a welcome break. And when Bettina Winslow proved purely by coincidence to be the owner of the favorite for the second race that made for all the better misdirection.'

'The red herring of favoritism served to draw attention from the more important fact that Masterton and Mrs Winslow had previously been husband and wife. And as a reporter you were in a position to highlight that coincidence, weren't you, Les? Take advantage of it?'

'Certainly. Especially when I was able to get an American outlet for my writing, that perfectly marvelous *National Onlooker*. I am quite a good newspaperman, you know. I could go far in journalism anywhere at all.'

'You should do a dandy job for the prison weekly,' said Martin Fine. 'Or the mental hospital gazette.'

'I don't think so!' Randall snapped. 'I don't think that's where my future lies.'

'Why weren't there any more Old Rosebud letters after the second death?' Jerry pursued.

'Well, you see, by now I was more determined than ever to complete the series, whatever happened to me after that. I halted the letters, feeling I'd pressed my luck on that score far enough.'

'And you did complete the series.'

'Yes,' said Randall with satisfaction. 'It was

fortunate that everyone was focusing attention on the owner of the favorite. My efforts to make everyone zero in on Martin as a logical target had borne more fruit that I could have hoped. While I cannot say my real victim did not suspect a thing, the fact that security protection wasn't centered on him made it far easier for me to get to him in the Belmont parking lot that afternoon. It didn't take but a moment.'

'That seems a dangerous place to commit murder, Les,' Jerry said. 'You might easily have been seen.'

'By that point, Jerry, I confess I was getting reckless. I didn't care what happened to me, so long as Engle died. If I actually had been determined to kill you, Martin, I can only suppose I would have failed. I suppose it's too much to ask that you should be grateful to me, Jerry. In my choice of third victim, I afforded you a chance to do your race-calling on national television. I've advanced both your television careers, haven't I, Martin? I gave you a script and Jerry a chance.'

'Oh, yeah,' said Fine, 'you're a regular public benefactor.'

'Once I had crushed the last vestige of life out of Engle, I assumed my luck would hold no longer, that I would be promptly caught, and what would it matter? I hadn't even considered the happy fact that several other possible suspects had been on the scene and bereft of alibis. But that day passed, no police dogged my heels, and I began to entertain the possibility of continued survival. A bonus. The idea cheered me. Perhaps I could go on my merry way as Les Randall and never be found out. Listening to you tonight, Jerry, I reconsidered my chances of carrying the deception any farther and decided it was time to call a halt. So there we are. Where do we go from here?'

'Where do *you* go from here is the question, Randall,' Martin Fine said.

'I think I have my options,' the reporter mused, seeming fully in control of himself now. 'It's up to you three, along with the police and the world at large, to decide if I belong in the ranks of crazy multiple killers. But it helped me no end to look like a crazy killer, and I assure you I am far less crazy than the killer I seemed.'

Donna spoke again, softly and unthreateningly, with a sense of horrified wonder. 'You killed all those people just because your father lost his job.'

'You haven't been listening!' Randall roared. He raised himself halfway out of his chair, then dropped back down again, holding his head as if trying desperately to keep control. 'No, no, I'm sorry. You've misunderstood. It's my fault. I haven't told you quite everything.' Randall gripped the edge of his chair now, and the maniacal glint returned to his eyes, the long-suppressed American intonations to his speech. 'Did you think those bastards just fired him? Just tried to ruin his career? A man of his gifts could have risen above that easily. But that wasn't enough for them. Their hatred took a different form.

'They hired a couple of strongarm brutes, one dead and the other imprisoned now or I'd have gone after them, too. Those two thugs grabbed my father, subdued him, and brought him to Van Ness Masterton, stripped him of his clothes and tied him naked to a bed in the Masterton house. Can you imagine the humiliation he must have felt? But even that is not all.

'There, the three of them, Masterton and his wife and Grant Engle, their playmate, took knives in their hands and threatened to perform on my father the same little operation that had mistakenly been performed on Blueskying. They were very convincing of their intention, filling the air with much talk of making the punishment fit what they thought was the crime. No, they didn't actually make my father a gelding. They only threatened it. Only! They only frightened him. Only! Only made a strong man into a weeping, pleading, shitting hulk, robbed him of all pride, of all self-respect, and ruined him forever. He was afraid and ashamed to tell anyone else, but helped by cheap booze he did gather the courage to tell me one memorable evening. He should have gone after them himself, but at least he gave me the chance to seek his revenge for him. He was a pitiful wreck, my father, ruined for any kind of decisive action. And he had been a considerable person. You have to believe that.'

Tears were rolling down his cheeks now. For a few moments there was silence in the room as he struggled to regain control.

As if by force of will, the killer in the chair became Les Randall again. 'There it is, Jerry,' he said, in a parody of his urbane drawl. 'How do you think it would play to the readers of the *National Onlooker*? Move a few copies in that checkstand queue?'

He stood up.

'Where are you going, Les?' Jerry asked.

'I'm not going anywhere.' He raised his arms, yawning and stretching. 'My, hasn't all this confession been taxing? I'm sure you have found it so, too. I feel the need of a little fresh air. You don't mind if I enjoy your view, do you, Martin?'

'Not at all,' Fine said. 'Enjoy, enjoy.' Randall walked toward the sliding door and stepped out onto the patio.

Jerry tensed and leaned forward, not sure what to do. Fine raised a calming hand. 'Relax. Where can he go?'

Answering the question in his own mind, Jerry jumped to his feet and lumbered after the journalist.

Randall was trotting toward the wall now, swinging one leg onto the top of it. Then he pulled himself up on both legs and stood there poised to jump. Jerry lunged desperately, threw his arms around Randall's waist and lifted him in the air, pulling him away from the wall and finally pinning him on the surface of the building's roof. For a moment they lay listening to each other's heavy breathing.

'Why couldn't you let me do it, Jerry? Why?'

'I'm really sorry, Les. But you could have killed somebody down there.'

Martin Fine was on the intercom to his security force below. The police would not be long coming.

'Let me up,' Randall panted. 'I'm not going anywhere.'

'You said that before.'

'I mean it this time. Please let me up, Jerry.'

Jerry gradually released the pressure but kept a warning hand on Randall's arm as the two of them rose to their feet. 'Sure, Les, just stay away from that wall.'

Moments later the doorbell rang, and a trio of police, two uniformed and one in plain clothes, entered the penthouse. Even Les Randall seemed glad and relieved to see them.

*　　*　　*

In their hotel room later, Donna said, 'Don't worry about it, Jerry. It's all over now.'

'Yeah, sure. But that cop had no call to chew me out the way he did. "We were already onto duh guy, Mr Brogan. We knew he was duh poipetratah and were just waitin' to make our move." Sure they were.'

'Maybe they were. Why not?'

'Maybe they were, but he accused me of putting innocent people in danger because I wanted to grandstand. Donna, I did my best to leave this case to the proper authorities. You know I did. And nobody was in any danger. I had that all figured out.'

'Well, there were the presumably innocent pedestrians down on Park Avenue he might have splattered on,' Donna pointed out. 'Stopping him then was the heroic part, Jerry. You might have gotten *yourself* killed if you hadn't timed it just right.'

'I'm glad there was a heroic part.' He drew her closer to him. 'They're probably right. I shouldn't have put you through all that, dangerous or not. But when he showed up like that, out of the blue, I felt I had to confront him. I just improvised.'

'I didn't mind. After all, I came to New York to go to the theater, didn't I?'

*   *   *

Back on the scene at Surfside Meadows, Jerry was over the less pleasant after-effects of the Old Rosebud case and was becoming freshly impressed with his brilliant detective work. He felt he should call his Surfside police contact, Lieutenant Wilmer Friend, and offer him a full account.

Friend listened politely. He probably knew it all already, so it wasn't reasonable to expect him to punctuate the story with interjections of 'Amazing!' or 'You don't say!' But Jerry thought he could have acted a bit more impressed.

'So I was right,' said Friend, after a pause to

be sure Jerry was finished.

'What do you mean you were right?'

'Didn't I tell you Denny Kilbride committed suicide?'

Photoset, printed and bound in Great Britain by
REDWOOD BURN LIMITED, Trowbridge, Wiltshire

0
61 8
62
38 63
39 64
40 65
41 66
42 117
43 11
4 11
120
12